# Skin Deep

# clearwater crossing

# Skin Deep

## laura peyton roberts

BANTAM BOOKS
NEW YORK • TORONTO • LONDON • SYDNEY • AUCKLAND

RL 5.8, age 12 and up
SKIN DEEP
A Bantam Book / June 1999

ISBN 0-553-49260-8

Published simultaneously in the United States and Canada.

Bantam Books are published by Bantam Books, a division of Random
House, Inc. Its trademark, consisting of the words "Bantam Books" and
the portrayal of a rooster, is Registered in U.S. Patent and Trademark
Office and in other countries. Marca Registrada. Bantam Books, 1540
Broadway, New York, New York 10036.

PRINTED IN THE UNITED STATES OF AMERICA

OPM   10   9   8   7   6   5   4   3   2   1

*For Margot and Ela*

The Lord does not look at the things man looks at. Man looks at the outward appearance, but the Lord looks at the heart.

1 Samuel 16:7b

# *One*

"Marry me, Leah," Miguel del Rios repeated. "Why not?"

Leah Rosenthal stared at him, unable to speak. Nothing in her life had prepared her for this moment—her boyfriend down on one knee in the busy St. Louis airport, his brown eyes boring into hers . . .

"You love me, don't you?" he asked.

One of his hands clutched a bouquet of flowers; the other extended a silver ring insistently in her direction. "Leah, for Pete's sake. Say something."

Leah opened her mouth to speak, but her lungs were so constricted she could barely catch her breath. Not even a whisper came out.

"Leah?"

Her hand went to her throat. Why couldn't she answer him? She felt as if she were choking. The airport around Miguel dissolved into a shimmering haze of white.

*Am I fainting?* she wondered, just as Miguel

faded into nothingness too and she woke up, bright California sunshine pouring through a gap in the hotel drapes, straight into her dazzled eyes.

*It was only a dream*, she realized, groaning.

Her fingertips found the red hair ribbon digging into the soft flesh of her throat and pulled it from beneath her head, where it had become trapped during a rough night's sleep. The narrow satin ribbon was tied in a long loop around her neck, and at the end of the loop Miguel's ring glimmered, throwing silvered sparks of sunlight deep into the shadowy room.

Leah turned her face toward the shadows, made out Nicole Brewster's open-mouthed profile in the bed next to hers, and almost groaned again. Somehow the sight of Nicole in her room made being in Hollywood feel completely, irrevocably real.

Beyond the sleeping blonde, the door of the adjoining room stood partly open. Jenna Conrad and Melanie Andrews were in there, presumably asleep as well, sharing similar accommodations. Leah would have preferred to room with Jenna, but by the time they had finally arrived at the hotel Friday night, she hadn't been in the mood to argue when Nicole had taken over and made the room assignments. She'd known Nicole's interest in sharing with her had more to do with wanting to be close to the modeling action than with friendship, but it just wasn't important enough to make a fuss about—especially not

2

when all four girls were going to be within shouting distance of each other anyway.

After the long plane ride from Missouri and the shuttle trip from LAX to the hotel, all Leah had wanted to do was get into bed and pull the covers over her head. The flight had been a four-hour ordeal of worrying and second-guessing herself while simultaneously trying to pretend nothing was wrong. By the time they'd landed, she'd been too exhausted even to comment on the amazingly wide concrete freeways, choked with red taillights, or the spraypainted graffiti adorning the signs and overpasses.

Because, to Leah's dismay, when Miguel had proposed in the airport, she'd been so taken by surprise that she'd never given him a straight answer. And while reality hadn't been an exact duplicate of her recent nightmare, it hadn't been so different, either.

"It's stupid to be separated when there's no need for it," he'd insisted, still on his knee. "All this talk about college has made me see that. Come on and marry me, Leah. Let's skip straight to the good part."

"You can't be serious," she'd finally gotten out, taking his hand and pulling him to his feet. "We're too young."

"Almost eighteen, and that's old enough. What do you say?"

"But—I—this is so sudden." There was no way she was skipping college and getting married so young. But how could she tell him that without hurting him? Would he ever forgive her?

"Announcing final boarding for Flight 384 to Los Angeles," an amplified voice had announced. "Final boarding now, through Gate C36."

Startled, Leah had glanced toward the gate and had seen her three girlfriends waiting, throwing anxious looks her way. She had been more tempted than ever not to get on the plane, but Nicole, in particular, had seemed ready to come unglued. And she *had* promised them a trip to California. . . .

"I—I have to go," she'd told Miguel, torn. "I wish I didn't, but I do."

"Just think about it," he'd urged, pressing the roses into one of her hands and his silver ring into the other. "Think about it and tell me when you get back."

"Miguel, I—"

His kiss had interrupted her protest. "When you get back," he'd repeated, half pushing her toward the gate.

*Why was he in such a hurry?* she wondered now, staring at his ring. *Why didn't he beg me to stay?*

Had he already guessed she was going to say no? Maybe he wanted to hear it in private, instead of with the entire female half of Eight Prime looking on. Not that they'd had a chance of hearing what was being said from that far away. The crowd had been so thick that Leah wasn't even sure how much they'd been able to see.

4

Everything that had happened after that was fuzzy. She barely remembered getting onto the plane, and taking off was a blur. But once they were off the ground, her friends had peppered her with questions about the meaning of Miguel's romantic and unexpected appearance.

"He just wanted to say good-bye," Leah had ad-libbed weakly, pressing her face to the window. "Look, isn't that the Missouri River?"

Jenna and Melanie had strained to see, but Nicole hadn't been so easily distracted.

"With a ring?" she'd asked skeptically, pointing to the pocket where Leah had slipped it. "On his knees?"

Leah's heart had beat faster. "He was just fooling around—having some fun, you know?" She'd taken the plain silver band from her pocket and handed it to Nicole. "Not exactly diamonds, see? He just wanted me to remember him by it while I was gone."

Now Leah sat up in the hotel bed and let Miguel's ring drop to the end of its ribbon, where it bounced against her chest. She had a feeling she wasn't going to do anything *but* remember him the entire weekend.

Nicole snorted in her sleep, and Leah froze. There was still no sound from the adjacent room, and she wanted to savor her privacy as long as she could before the craziness of the U.S. Girls contest began.

Keeping a wary eye on Nicole, Leah wondered if her friends had believed her fib about Miguel. She didn't like to lie, but she'd do it again if it kept him from being embarrassed. She only wished she'd had time to come up with a better story!

Leah swung her legs out of bed and tried to stop worrying. *Miguel was just saying good-bye*, she rehearsed determinedly.

That was her story, and she was sticking to it.

Jenna walked hesitantly to the registration desk in the lobby, where the girls had checked in and received four room keys the night before.

"Hi. Uh, excuse me. Could you tell me where the Hearts for God rally is?" she asked a red-vested clerk behind the counter.

"The Empire Room," he said, leaning out to point through the wide, marble-tiled atrium.

Jenna's eyes followed his finger across the lobby, where early-morning sunlight blazed through the front windows, forming puddles of light on the highly polished floor. Red leather chairs and potted palms were scattered across the enormous space, arranged in casual groupings. And on the other side of the lobby the marble flooring continued, stretching down a wide corridor.

"That way?" Jenna asked uncertainly, pointing a finger of her own.

"Yes. Then down the escalator and to your left."

Jenna strode off toward the hallway, wondering if Melanie and Nicole were awake yet. Leah had been in the shower when Jenna had climbed out of bed and slipped silently into jeans and a sweatshirt. Jenna had paused only long enough to brush her teeth and comb the tangles out of her long brown hair before she'd grabbed her room key and taken the elevator down to the lobby.

She'd probably have looked for the rally right off anyway, but that Saturday morning she was even more in need of inspiration than usual. She still felt so awful about betraying Caitlin's trust the night before that she half wished she'd never left home. How could she have told Peter about Caitlin's crush on his brother after her sister had specifically asked her not to? And then to have to leave town with Caitlin in tears and everything so unresolved . . .

Feeling horribly guilty, Jenna hurried toward the Empire Room, noticing as she went that the back side of the lobby was glass as well, with an elaborate swimming pool and entertainment deck outdoors. Lounge chairs were arranged in rows, as though they might actually be used later in the day.

*Lounge chairs in January!* she thought, brightening a little. *Amazing.*

The Empire Room was even more amazing. Bigger than the CCHS gymnasium back home, it boasted fancy patterned carpeting, beige wallpaper, and huge chandeliers. The front part of the room was open and level with the entry doors, but about a third of the way back, a gleaming brass railing marked the drop-off to a second, much larger level. Row upon row of chairs filled the sunken portion, facing a stage at the far end.

At that early hour the stage was still empty, but the room was far from vacant. In contrast to the relative desolation of the upstairs lobby, this spot was packed with teens and their youth advisors, greeting each other, laughing, and all trying to talk at once. Tables laden with pastries and juice lined the wall to one side of the entry doors, and Jenna felt her stomach rumble.

*Don't even think about it*, she told herself, turning and weaving through the crowd in the opposite direction. *You're having breakfast with Leah.*

Which reminded her she had to hurry. Glancing nervously at her watch, she joined the crowd in front of the tables under the REGISTRATION banner, falling in behind a pair of giggling girls and their suitcases. The two kept their heads close together as they talked, emphasizing the resemblance between them.

*Sisters*, Jenna thought with another stab of remorse over her falling-out with Caitlin.

Looking around, she realized the girls weren't the only ones with luggage. Bags and backpacks dangled from the wrists of otherwise occupied hands and cluttered a section of wall between two open doors. It seemed people were so excited to join the rally they didn't even want to check into their rooms first. The meeting hall was full of energy, and Jenna found herself shifting from foot to foot, eager to reach the front of the line. At last it was her turn.

"Are you checking in?" a kind-looking woman asked, her pencil poised over a thick roster of names.

"Uh, not exactly." Jenna glanced from the woman seated at the table to the brightly colored inspirational T-shirts and posters pinned to the wall behind her. She wished she *were* checking in, she realized. Not that she didn't want to hang out with her friends, but the rally looked so fun. "I was wondering, um, well—is it possible to come to some of the events if I'm not actually registered?"

Briefly Jenna explained her situation: She was really there for the U.S. Girls contest but hated missing the rally when she was so close. "I'm hoping I'll have some time to at least drop by and check things out. The problem is, I probably won't know when I'll be free until it happens."

"Here, take these." The woman pushed four printed slips of paper across the table. "They're guest passes. If you and your friends find some spare time, you can visit for free."

"Thanks!" Jenna said, picking up the passes. "Thanks a lot. There's one more thing I was wondering. Could I get Fire & Water tickets? I mean, I would pay for them, but are there any left? Do you know where I can buy them?"

She held her breath for the answer. Fire & Water

wasn't just an extremely popular Christian rock band, it was her new favorite. She'd practically worn out their debut CD, and she'd only had it a few weeks.

"The show's sold out, but we did hold back some tickets. The person who's in charge of that isn't here yet, though. Try back in an hour."

Jenna checked her watch and felt her heart miss a beat. Was that really the time? She was going to be late for Leah's breakfast!

"I'll do that," she said hurriedly. "Thanks. You've been really nice."

Clutching her guest passes, Jenna wheeled around and ran out of the Empire Room, taking the escalator up to the lobby. Her sneakers squeaked as she bolted over the polished expanse of marble toward the elevators on the other side. She skidded to a stop in front of them, sweat tickling her hairline.

"Come *on*," she muttered, repeatedly punching the button with the up arrow on it.

But her thoughts were still back at the rally. What if they sold out of Fire & Water tickets before she returned? What if the U.S. Girls contest kept her so busy that she missed the entire thing? What if—

*What if you take the stairs before Leah kills you?* she interrupted herself, running for the stairwell.

"Jeans? You're wearing *jeans?*"

Nicole's outraged voice cut through a soft, fuzzy blanket of sleep, assaulting Melanie's ears. Exhausted, she tried to make sense of the fact that Nicole had invaded her dreams.

"If they don't like it . . . ," Leah replied testily, her meaning clear. "Anyway, they're a jeans company, so what's the problem?"

"It's just that, well, I mean . . . ," Nicole sputtered. "It's the opening breakfast! I was going to wear something fancy."

"Go ahead. No one's stopping you."

And then Melanie remembered. She wasn't dreaming; she was in California.

Sitting up abruptly, she discovered that she was the last to awake. Jenna's unmade bed was empty, and from the brittle edge to Leah's voice, Melanie had a feeling Nicole had been awake a long time. She smiled gratefully as she slid out of bed and padded barefoot to the sliding glass door to her balcony—she didn't know how Leah had gotten stuck with Nicole, she was only glad it wasn't her.

Parting the heavy drapes, Melanie silently undid the lock and slid the big glass door open, making a gap just large enough to get through sideways. The low-slung sun washed the skin exposed by her nightgown as she took her first deep breath of cool morning air. There was enough of a chill to remind Melanie it was still the middle of January, but it was early in the morning, and the day promised to get hotter. Besides, compared to what Clearwater Crossing had endured for the past month, the weather felt like

11

heaven. Melanie could barely wait to get out and see the sights of Hollywood!

Putting both hands on the cold iron railing of the balcony, she leaned out as far as she could, toward the noisy, sprawling city below. Eleven stories beneath her, rooftops of varying heights and colors crowded together in the sunshine, lining streets that beelined toward the distant smog-veiled hills. A parade of cars and tour buses rumbled impatiently down the pavement, shaking the town to life. And rising above it all were the palm trees. Impossibly tall and thin, they added exclamation points wherever they grew, as if to say, "Yes! This is really California!"

Letting her gaze drop, Melanie traced the smooth loop of asphalt curving from the road to the hotel entrance. She watched as a limousine pulled up and disappeared beneath the garnet-colored canopy. Then another, brighter, flash of red caught her eye—a BMW was pulling off the main road into the parking lot.

*Jesse*, she thought, her pulse quickening.

But of course that was ridiculous. Jesse was back in Missouri, where she'd left him.

She winced at the potential double meaning. She hadn't actually *left* Jesse, she'd just broken off whatever that mess was that they'd gotten into. It wasn't working out between them, so she'd definitely done the right thing.

She just hadn't expected him to take it so hard.

Now, remembering the devastated look on his face when she'd handed back the porcelain angel he'd given her, she was surprised by how awful she felt. She had expected to bruise his ego a little, but that was all. The way he'd acted, though, was more like she'd broken his heart. He'd made her feel so guilty that for a moment, right before Leah had pulled up to collect her for the trip, Melanie had almost relented.

She took a deep breath of the California air, savoring the mixture of strange smells. *I made the right decision*, she reassured herself. *Not only that, my timing was perfect.* A change of scenery was just the thing to wipe the entire affair from her mind.

She glanced at the BMW again, a small red toy parked far below. A young, brown-haired guy climbed out, and Melanie's heart squeezed painfully.

She *had* made the right decision. Hadn't she?

*Of course I did*, she thought, spinning quickly away from the view. *No more thinking about Jesse!*

Melanie had barely stepped back into the room when Jenna stumbled through the door from the hall, her creamy cheeks scarlet and her chest heaving. Almost simultaneously, Nicole barged through the door of the adjoining room, her outfit coordinated down to her red toenail polish. Her turquoise eyes went wild when she saw Melanie and Jenna.

"Do you know what time it is?" she demanded, looking from one to the other.

Jenna had collapsed on her unmade bed, her hair spilling over the edge to the floor. "Stairs," she got out between gasps, not even trying to answer Nicole.

Melanie glanced at the clock radio as she walked to her own bed and picked up a hairbrush. "Eight-fifteen."

"That's right! Eight-fifteen!" Nicole repeated hysterically. "We're supposed to be downstairs at eight-thirty!"

"Are you sure? I thought it was nine."

Nicole seemed about to have a panic attack when Leah walked into the room. Despite the fact that she was the contestant, Leah looked as relaxed as Nicole was hyper, as underdressed as Nicole was over.

"Oh, good!" Jenna said, sitting up. "You're wearing jeans too. I'm just going to shower and put on a cooler top. I'll be ready in ten minutes."

"You're *both* wearing jeans?" Nicole said disbelievingly.

She had on a very snug, low-cut red sweater and a white skirt slit to the top of her thigh. Her hair had been tormented into shiny corkscrew curls, piled on top of her head with rhinestone clips, and sprayed into complete immobility. But her hairdo was nothing compared to her makeup. Bright green eye shadow cut a swath up to darkly penciled brows, and blood-red lipstick emphasized her paleness in a way that definitely wasn't flattering. Strappy white sandals lifted her heels about three inches off the ground; her

14

sense of appropriateness seemed to have floated off much farther.

"I'll wear jeans too," Melanie announced on impulse.

"You guys are *killing* me!" Nicole declared, stomping one pedicured foot. "Am I the only person who's excited to be here, or what?"

"You're not even going to *try* your sweet roll?" Jenna asked Nicole incredulously. "They're really good."

Nicole made a face, imagining the amount of fat packed into that little blob of dough. "You want it? Go ahead."

"I never eat pastry either," another contestant confided from across the table they were sharing as Jenna speared Nicole's roll with a fork. "Fruit is a much healthier breakfast, don't you think?"

"Absolutely!" Nicole returned emphatically, even though she didn't usually eat fruit, either. She didn't usually eat at all, if she could avoid it, but she didn't want to go into that with a stranger and her three friends.

"Much better for the complexion, too," the other girl continued. "Although you obviously don't need to worry about that," she added for Jenna's benefit.

"Nope," Jenna agreed, munching happily. "My

whole family has good skin. We're just blessed that way, I guess."

*You're going to be blessed with big thighs, too, the way you're going,* Nicole thought sourly, wishing Jenna would at least *pretend* to be a light eater for once. The way she devoured sweets was definitely her most unattractive habit.

"This stupid badge is in the way of everything. I can't even use my knife," Leah complained, glancing impatiently at the large red-white-and-blue cardboard name tag pinned to her pink shirt. "Do you think they could make them any bigger?"

"They were probably trying to keep it to one tree apiece," Melanie joked, provoking laughter from Leah and Jenna.

Nicole squeezed her eyes shut, mortified. Ungrateful Leah had been moaning about her contestant's badge from the moment they'd pinned it on her. Who cared if it was a little big? What Nicole wouldn't give to be wearing one just like it! She opened her eyes in time to catch the slight, sympathetic smile of the contestant across the table, whose badge read KATE MATTHEWS, WISCONSIN.

At least someone understood! Here they were, at the most exciting event of any of their lives, and all Nicole's friends could do was eat pastry and complain. *I've never seen a less appreciative group,* she thought, making a point of returning Kate's smile.

"Welcome to the U.S. Girls national modeling

16

search finals," a woman's voice boomed from the podium at the front of the room, drowning out the din of young voices and clattering silverware.

The contestants and their guests were being served in a banquet hall that contained thirty round, white-draped tables crowned with spiky centerpieces of exotic flowers. Two similarly decorated rectangular tables at the front of the room were occupied by eight judges. From a podium between the tables, one of those judges had just addressed them. Now she adjusted the volume on the microphone and assumed a more cultivated tone.

"I'm happy to see you all today," she continued. "As you know, finalists from fifty states were invited here to compete on this Martin Luther King Day weekend. On Monday night just five of them will be selected as U.S. Girls, winning scholarships and roles in a national advertising campaign. We have a full slate of events planned over the next three days, so we'll be speaking to the contestants very briefly if they'll meet us next door after breakfast." She pointed toward a doorway into a smaller adjoining room. "And to help move things along, we need contestants *only*, please."

"That's the head judge," Nicole heard Kate whisper to her friends. "That guy on her right is her second."

Nicole sat farther forward in her seat, memorizing their features.

"We don't have a formal presentation this morning—we're saving that for lunchtime. So once again, let me just say how pleased we are to have you as our guests here in Los Angeles. We hope this will be an experience you remember for years to come."

"Bound to be," Leah muttered cryptically, earning an amused snicker from Melanie.

The judge took her seat again to applause from the audience. Nicole applauded the loudest, hoping the woman might look her way, but the talking and clanking of dishes resumed immediately, and she was drowned out in the hubbub.

"What's after this?" she asked Leah.

"Pool party," Leah replied, finally getting around to trying her pastry. "Ooh, these *are* good."

Nicole shook her head, unable to believe that a contestant in a modeling contest would even consider eating such junk the weekend she was going to compete. At the same moment, though, she caught a glimpse of someone walking by in the hall outside and pastry suddenly became the last thing on her mind.

"Matt Damon!" she squealed, jumping out of her seat.

"Where?" everyone else at the table demanded.

"In the hall! I just saw him go by." Nicole dug frantically through her overstuffed tote bag for the autograph book and pen she'd brought in case of just such an occurrence.

The other girls were on their feet, ready to bolt wherever she pointed.

All but Leah. "Was he wearing a white jacket, by any chance?"

"Um, yeah. Yeah, I think he was." Nicole's fingers closed around the smooth plastic barrel of her pen.

Leah laughed and pointed toward the far front corner of the room. "There's a resemblance, I'll grant you. But I kind of doubt Matt Damon is busing our breakfast dishes."

"What?" Nicole spun around, mortified to see the handsome blond she had just announced as an actor pick up a gray plastic tub and begin collecting dirty dishes. "But, but—" she sputtered.

"He just came in the other door," Jenna explained, pointing to a side door down the hall from their table.

"It's the hair," one of Kate's friends said good-naturedly. "He had me going for a second too."

Melanie laughed and sat down. "If we'd taken maybe a second to think about it, we would have realized that the chances of seeing a star that big in the hotel are zero. Maybe less. I think you can drop the celebrity watch, Nicole."

Nicole tried to hide her irritation behind a dignified facade as she took her seat again. "You never know," she said stiffly, not in the least convinced.

She was expecting amazing things that weekend, and there was no way she was going to let Melanie

Andrews or anybody else rain on her parade. God wouldn't have sent her to L.A. if something incredible wasn't going to happen—and Nicole remained certain he had sent her. How else could she explain Leah's unexpected invitation to the contest, the surprise gift of a suitcase from her parents, or the fact that she'd been allowed to take the trip even after she and her sister had been busted for toilet-papering some junior-high boy's house? She wouldn't have risked permanently offending her best friend, Courtney, by taking the trip without her if she wasn't sure of great things.

*This is the weekend that will change my life*, she thought happily, forgetting the Matt Damon incident. Before she left for home on Tuesday morning, she'd be discovered and offered a modeling job. Perhaps not for U.S. Girls, but the contest judges must have all sorts of other connections. Not to mention that Hollywood was a big place—she could be noticed anywhere, by anyone. At a contest event, at the pool, on a bus . . .

Nicole smiled, barely able to keep her good news to herself as she imagined her triumphant return to Clearwater Crossing, a modeling contract in hand. Courtney would forgive her then, all right. And Jesse . . . well . . . so what if they were just friends now? She'd still make him eat his heart out.

*Fame and fortune, here I come!*

# Two

Leah shut the hotel room door hard behind her as she returned from the postbreakfast meeting.

"Don't look for me for the next couple of hours," she said irritably as three startled heads swung her way. "All the contestants have to go to a rules and information meeting downstairs now."

Melanie and Jenna were poring over tourist brochures at a small round table in front of Leah's balcony door. Melanie put hers down on the table. "What? Then what was that meeting you just went to?"

"The meeting to tell us to come to the meeting, I guess," Leah said disgustedly. "This bites."

"I thought we were going to a pool party!" Nicole wailed, straightening up from the open suitcase on her bed with a bikini in each hand. "That's what you said!"

"Apparently *you* guys are going to a pool party. If I'm lucky I'll get to drop in for the last hour."

"But the schedule—" Jenna began.

Leah shook her head and plopped down on her

bed, already tired. The motion caused Miguel's hidden ring to bounce beneath her shirt, and she put her hand over it self-consciously. "I wouldn't pay too much attention to that schedule. From what the judges just told us, it's more of a guideline. There's a lot of stuff we contestants have to do while everyone else is having fun."

"That's awful!" Jenna said. "It's your trip. You ought to have more fun than anyone!"

Leah nodded, knowing her friend meant well. She had already heard enough about the youth rally to guess that Jenna wouldn't have any trouble filling her free time.

"I won't go to the pool party," Nicole announced tragically, putting down her bathing suits. "I'll go to the meeting with you. Don't worry, Leah. I'll keep you company, no matter what."

Nicole obviously thought she was making the ultimate sacrifice, so Leah tried not to show her dismay at the thought of spending three uninterrupted days with her. That kind of togetherness would wear her out under the best of conditions, but the way Nicole had been carrying on so far, it was unimaginable. Melanie and Jenna seemed perfectly content with the fact that they were only along for the ride, but Nicole . . .

There was no doubt in Leah's mind that Nicole was working on some sort of modeling agenda, although she hadn't yet figured out exactly what it was. Surely Nicole didn't expect to wangle her way into the contest at this late date?

"Thanks, Nicole," Leah said slowly. "I appreciate the offer, but the meeting's for contestants only."

"That's so unfair!" said Nicole, looking crushed.

"Well, I'm sure you'll have a good time at the pool party. I think half the judges are going to be out there to make sure everyone's guests have fun."

"Really?"

Leah had to choke back a laugh as Nicole's eyes bugged out. A moment later she was digging frantically through her suitcase again.

"Looking forward to taking home a tan?" Melanie asked her with obvious amusement.

*She's definitely looking forward to taking home something,* Leah thought. *And I'd really love to know what.*

"I'll take four, please," Jenna said anxiously. "Do you have four left all together?"

"I'm sorry. What?" The guy behind the table put a hand up to his ear. The Hearts for God rally had become so loud that a person had to shout to be heard.

Jenna repeated her request, more forcefully, and after some shuffling the man came up with four seats side by side.

"They're pretty far in the back," he said. "But you're lucky to get them at all. The theater's not enormous, so you'll still be able to see."

"Just so long as I can hear," Jenna said. "How much are they?"

"A hundred and twenty for four."

Jenna blinked, then opened her wallet and took out six twenties. She had known the tickets wouldn't be cheap, but multiplied by four they added up fast. Luckily, her parents had given her the money before she left.

"With Leah taking you on the whole trip for free, the least we can do is treat for the concert," her mother had said. "Assuming you can fit it in, that is."

Now Jenna zipped the precious tickets into the smallest pocket of her backpack, praying she'd have the chance to use them. *If not, I can always resell them*, she thought. It would kill her, but at least her mother wouldn't lose her money.

"I'd also like two of those T-shirts," she told the ticket seller, pointing to the design she liked best: a stylized burst of red-orange flame on a shirt the cool blue green of water. The pricey souvenirs were coming out of her own money, but after she'd paid for the shirts—one for her and one for Peter—she suddenly had an idea.

"Can I please get one more?" she asked, thinking of Caitlin. A peace offering couldn't hurt.

With the three shirts tucked safely into the main pouch of her backpack, Jenna turned to go. Nicole and Melanie were probably already at the pool party, wondering where she was.

24

*No, they know where I am. And besides, it's not like they're waiting around for me. I could stay a couple more minutes. . . .*

Hesitating on the landing behind the sunken area of chairs, Jenna wondered what she'd be missing when she left. The noise in the room had suddenly died down, apparently in anticipation of some impending event. Most of the chairs facing the stage were full, and though there was still a lot of talking and laughing, it was of the hushed, clipped sort that could be broken off on a moment's notice. Jenna walked over to the brass railing that divided the two levels.

"What's on next?" she asked a red-haired girl also lingering to watch.

"Sandy Salvatore," the girl replied. "She's supposed to talk about living like you mean it, or something like that."

"Oh! Oh, I love her!" Jenna said. "Did you read her book?"

The girl shook her head. "Should I have?"

"Well, *I* really liked it." Jenna hesitated at the railing, hating to miss a speaker who inspired her so much. "Are you here by yourself?"

"No. My sister's here somewhere." The redhead rolled her eyes. "Sisters! Who needs 'em?"

"Did you have a fight?" Jenna guessed.

The girl nodded. "She's so touchy! But it wasn't that big a deal—it'll blow over by lunch."

"That's good." Jenna wondered if her new friend realized how lucky she was to be able to say that.

"My name's Julie, by the way."

"I'm Jenna. And I have five sisters myself, so I know what you're going through."

"Five!" Julie looked heavenward. "Wow, there's an entry for my gratitude journal. One's all I can handle."

Jenna smiled, though the discussion had only renewed her heartache over Caitlin. "It can be pretty tough sometimes, but without my sisters, I wouldn't even know who I am. They're part of you, you know?"

Julie's eyebrows rose in recognition. "Yeah."

Applause erupted below. A man was approaching the microphone onstage, presumably to announce the speaker.

"Hey, do you want to find seats together?" Julie offered. "It didn't sound so fun before, but since you liked the book . . ."

"Well . . ." Jenna toyed with the gold cross around her neck, trying to decide. There was no question what she'd prefer to do, but would Nicole and Melanie be mad if she didn't show up at the pool?

Then Sandy Salvatore walked onto the stage, and Jenna's mind was made up. If ever her spirits needed a lift, it was now. Besides, her friends were perfectly capable of entertaining themselves.

"I see two chairs over there," she told Julie, pointing.

*     *     *

"I don't know what makes you so sure we aren't going to see any celebrities," Nicole said from her perch on the edge of a hotel lounge chair. "There must be stars who come here to work sometimes who don't have homes in L.A."

Melanie shook her head without bothering to sit up. The late-morning air was warm enough for bathing suits, but barely, and she didn't want to disturb the sunlight pooled on her baby-oiled skin. "Why don't you go check the bar again? Brad Pitt is probably just sitting there waiting for you."

"You don't have to be sarcastic." Nicole stood up and made a production of stretching her bikini-clad body.

*On the contrary*, Melanie thought, adjusting her dark glasses. *The way you're acting today, sarcasm is mandatory.*

She and Nicole had never been close, and the fact that Nicole had had a totally futile crush on Jesse while he was chasing Melanie hadn't done much to bolster their relationship. Nicole and Jesse apparently had some sort of understanding now, and Nicole and Melanie had likewise called a truce—but that didn't make them buddies.

*It's a good thing she wasn't in the car when Leah picked me up Friday night*, Melanie thought. *Who knows what she would have made of Jesse being there?*

Jenna and Leah must have wondered, of course,

27

but they'd been mature enough not to mention it. Melanie had returned the favor to Leah by pretending to believe her story about Miguel "just saying good-bye" at the airport. If that was a good-bye, it was the most elaborate one Melanie had ever seen. Whatever those two were up to was their business, though. They'd spill it when they were ready.

"I'm going for another diet soda," Nicole announced, slipping her feet into fancy mesh mules and pulling on a nearly transparent cover-up. "Do you want one?"

"No, you go ahead."

*Please*, Melanie added silently, watching in disbelief as Nicole strutted off, her head and shoulders thrown so far back it was a miracle she could see well enough to avoid falling down. Propping herself up on her elbows, Melanie watched as Nicole ignored the sparkling pool and headed for the outdoor bar. Instead of taking the short route to her right, however, she walked all the way around the pool to her left—directly past the table where the U.S. Girls officials were keeping an eye on their guests from beneath a white canvas umbrella.

*They must think she's crazy!*

Nicole had already made that trip at least three times, returning the same way, and the last two sodas she'd picked up still rested conspicuously beneath her lounge chair, sweating in the sun. Melanie knew Nicole had wanted to win the U.S. Girls preliminaries in Missouri, but if she was trying to impress the judges now it was more than a little too late.

*Let it go*, Melanie thought, shaking her head. She could only hope the judges were sufficiently distracted by the rest of the crowd not to notice what a fool Nicole was making of herself.

Most of the hundred and fifty guests associated with the U.S. Girls contest were there that morning, along with other hotel occupants attempting to enjoy what Melanie had been told was unseasonably gorgeous weather. A rowdy group of guys had taken over the section of deck surrounding the diving board, and from the snippets of conversation that had carried her way, Melanie suspected them of playing hooky from the youth conference.

*Who could blame them?* she thought, comparing the turquoise appeal of the pool to an imagined series of dry, preachy lectures.

One of the guys caught her looking.

"Cannonball six!" he shouted, jumping onto the diving board. A moment later a terrific splash broke the surface of the previously undisturbed water, throwing drops of liquid crystal everywhere.

*Oh, wow. I'm so impressed.* Melanie rolled her eyes and lowered her original estimate of their ages by several years.

Then a smile snuck onto her lips. *Of course, if I could get him to do that again when Nicole is walking back . . .*

She could only imagine the shrieking.

"Is this seat taken?" A male voice surprised her from her other side.

Melanie turned to see a brown-haired guy in baggy swim trunks standing beside Nicole's vacant lounge.

"Strangely enough, that's why there's a towel on top and all that junk underneath," she replied, more curtly than she'd intended.

Did every guy in California have to remind her of Jesse? This one even smiled the same way—that unbearably self-satisfied smirk that said he was sure she wanted him badly.

"Actually, I saw your friend leave," he admitted. "But if the seat was full when she came back . . ."

Melanie could barely keep from laughing at such a blatant—not to mention clumsy—attempt to pick her up. This guy was starting to make Nicole look like good company.

"Sorry," Melanie said, matching him smirk for smirk.

But watching the view from behind as he walked off to try his charms somewhere else, she wondered why she'd been so hasty. He *was* kind of good-looking, and there were a lot more girls around than guys. Just because he reminded her of Jesse . . .

*Jesse, Jesse, Jesse!* she cursed silently, disgusted with herself. *You weren't going to think about him anymore!*

She scrambled restlessly out of her lounge chair

and stood beside it, at a loss. Jenna had apparently decided to stay at the rally, Leah was still in her meeting, and hanging out with Nicole was starting to feel like baby-sitting Barbie on a bad hair day. When Melanie had been invited to California, she hadn't much cared what she'd do there, but she'd also assumed it would be more exciting than hanging around the hotel, especially when there were so many other things to see.

Universal Studios was only five miles up the freeway, for example, but touring it was supposed to take all day. Disneyland was where she really wanted to go—except that it was a half-hour drive in the opposite direction. The hotel shuttle went to Hollywood Boulevard for free, though, and there were tons of things to see there: the Walk of Fame, the wax museum, Mann's Chinese Theater. . . .

*Of course U.S. Girls is supposed to take us to the boulevard on Monday, and there's no point seeing it twice when I could be doing something else.*

But what? That was the problem. She couldn't very well take off on her own with Leah supposed to show up any minute.

Melanie snapped her towel out over her lounge chair, smoothing out every crease before she lay down on her stomach, ignoring the scene at the pool.

*All this sitting around with Nicole is making me crazy,* she thought sulkily. *If things don't get more interesting soon, I will take off on my own.*

# Three

Jenna leaned back in her banquet chair, wondering if her eyes were really glazing over or if it only felt that way. Melanie and Leah looked as bored as she was, and even Nicole was squirming.

"Is this thing endless, or what?" one of the other girls at their table whispered. There were slight but definite nods of agreement all around.

If the luncheon presentation was supposed to show what a young and exciting company U.S. Girls was— like the judges said—then the people who'd put it together had badly missed the mark. Things had started out agreeably enough, with a fantastic Chinese chicken salad, but then the slide show had started. The show that was now sliding into its second hour . . .

"I think my brain is numb," Leah said, just barely lowering her voice.

"It *is* a lot of information," Nicole admitted.

"Do they expect you to know all this stuff?" Melanie asked Leah. "I mean, is that part of the deal or something?"

Leah's hazel eyes widened, while the other contestant at the table looked downright panic-stricken. Kate and her group were seated elsewhere, but an equally pretty blonde and three members of her family had joined them.

"I should have taken notes!" she moaned as the slides finally came to an end. Her words were nearly drowned out by polite applause.

"I don't think so," Jenna said soothingly. "There's nothing in the schedule about a quiz."

"I told you that schedule's not worth the paper it's printed on," Leah reminded her darkly. "Even so, I'm pretty sure they don't expect us to memorize forty random flow charts."

"Shhh!" Nicole shushed them, pointing at the podium. The head judge was taking the microphone.

"I hope you all enjoyed that," the woman said.

Jenna joined in the second round of perfunctory applause, hoping it meant they were almost out of there. Julie had told her about an afternoon breakout session at the rally, and she really wanted to get back. It wasn't impossible that Leah would be willing to see what the rally was about, since it was taking place right there in the hotel. . . .

"This concludes our lunch," the head judge continued, smoothing back a stray strand of overbleached hair. "We will take a half-hour break, and then our practice hair and makeup sessions will begin."

"Makeup?" Nicole repeated, perking up noticeably.

"Each contestant will meet with our hair and makeup artists to try out a few new looks, and wardrobe areas will be assigned in anticipation of the poise portion of the contest tonight. Guests are welcome to watch if they like, with the understanding that the process is likely to take several hours."

"I don't mind!" Nicole said quickly. "However long it takes is fine with me."

"You guys really want to go?"

Leah's tone made Jenna think it would be okay to say no. But Nicole nodded eagerly, and so did Melanie.

Jenna forced a smile and added her nod to the others. If that was what everyone wanted to do . . .

*So much for the rally*, she thought, trying not to be selfish. *After all, if it wasn't for Leah, I wouldn't even be here.*

"Do you have any idea where we're supposed to go?" Melanie asked Leah as the four girls entered a long, unattractive room.

Unlike the other areas of the hotel, which were deluxe in every way, the room they had just walked into was bleak and unfinished, with exposed ducts and pipes hugging the raw white walls. Girls crowded the alleylike space, flocking to the makeup tables and mirrors that lined one side, their voices echoing off the hard surfaces. Melanie wondered how many of them had decided to forgo the half-hour break after lunch and hurried directly to the makeup area instead.

"This place is a zoo," Leah said, sounding awed for the first time since they'd arrived in L.A. "Can you believe all this fuss about makeup? I barely even wore any when I won in Missouri."

"I keep telling you that was a miracle," Nicole insisted, rushing forward. "I'm glad they're going to make you wear some this time."

"I think you look pretty without makeup," Jenna said loyally.

Melanie glanced from Jenna's scrubbed-clean face to Nicole's overliberal makeup job and shook her head. *Something in the middle might be nice.*

Nicole had showered again after the pool party, leaving her shoulder-length hair straight and putting on fresh clothes for the lunch presentation. She'd changed clothes again afterward, pulling a seemingly unlimited wardrobe from all the luggage she'd brought. Now she wore a lime green sleeveless top with a flowered miniskirt, and she'd finally managed to badger poor Leah into wearing a skirt as well.

Melanie looked down at her own blue jeans and smiled as she followed the others. Normally she'd have dressed up more, but Nicole was being such a prima donna that refusing to change her clothes was the most fun she'd had so far.

"I see your name!" Jenna cried, running to an open place at the makeup table.

Apparently there were too many contestants to set up separate tables for each. Instead, a continuous line of gray folding tables had been erected against one wall, with fifty stand-up makeup mirrors plugged in side by side. A chair waited in front of each mirror, and taped to the wall above the chair Jenna had run to was the familiar red-white-and-blue sign: LEAH ROSENTHAL, MISSOURI.

"This must be the place," Leah said, plopping down. "I wonder where you guys are supposed to sit."

A number of folding metal chairs lined the opposite wall, many of them already occupied. "Over there, it looks like," Melanie said with a nod toward some empty ones.

"No way!" Nicole exclaimed. "How am I supposed to see anything way over there?"

"I don't know how much there'll be to see . . . ," Leah began, trailing off at an incredulous look from Nicole. "Well, all the *other* guests are sitting over there," she said defensively.

"I'll stand," Nicole said, crowding in behind Leah's chair as though she were the makeup artist. "This is so exciting! Do you think all this makeup is for you?"

Before Leah could answer, a harassed-looking woman with watches on both wrists bustled up and took over.

"No, that's my kit," she said, motioning for Nicole to give her some room. "You girls will get some free products, but those aren't them."

Nicole looked far more disappointed than Leah.

"Okay, so you're Leah, right?" the woman asked. "I'm Kay. Are you ready?" She checked one of her watches. "I've got five of you girls to take care of, so we need to move this along."

"Five!" Leah exclaimed. "Do you have to do our makeup for all the contest events, too?"

"Well, yes and no. We'll come up with a makeup plan today. I'll give you the products and colors we decide on, and I'll show you how to apply them. I can't be doing you girls individually for every segment of the contest, though, so you need to pay attention. That way you can do most of your own face when the competitions start, and I'll just pick up the details."

"I'll do my own," Leah said. "In fact, we can skip this if you want. I only really like mascara and lipstick anyway, so I don't see why I should add to your heart attack by changing my routine now."

"How about because you want to win?" Nicole said, butting in. "When you're up on a stage, no one's going to see that trace of mascara you wear."

"She's right," Kay said with a sideways glance at Nicole. Nicole absolutely beamed. "We can do something that from a distance will look pretty minimal, but if you want the judges to see your features, you have to paint them up—"

"Why would you want to do something minimal?" Nicole interrupted. "Come on, Leah. This is your chance to do something amazing!"

Kay looked Nicole's way again—longer this time—before returning her gaze to Leah. "You only live once. On the other hand, 'amazing' is in the eye of the beholder."

Melanie had to swallow a snort of laughter as she and Jenna retreated to the folding chairs across the narrow room.

Nicole didn't even seem to realize she'd just been insulted. "You are so right!" she agreed, nodding. "Absolutely."

"Just . . . do whatever you want," Leah told Kay. "I'll try to pay attention so I can do it myself later."

"Don't worry," said Nicole, still hovering. "I ought to be able to help you with anything you forget." She turned an obsequious smile on Kay. "Makeup's kind of a hobby of mine."

Melanie's lips pressed together as she waited for the zinger from Kay, but the makeup woman restrained herself somehow.

*She should have seen her this morning,* Melanie thought, half disappointed Kay had missed it. Nicole's afternoon look was demure compared to what she'd started out with.

"Okay now, Leah, just relax," Nicole said, as if she were about to perform surgery instead of simply interfere with the makeup woman. "It's hard to put makeup on a stiff face. Right, Kay?"

"Um, right. Do you think you could stand over there?" Kay asked, pointing to the floor a couple of feet away.

"Sure." Nicole moved to the spot, then immediately stepped back toward the table. "You know, jewel tones are great, and I really think Leah has the coloring to pull them off. You're the expert, but . . ." She pointed to the pots of lipstick in Kay's tray. "Don't you have something a little more berry?"

"Nicole'll be lucky if that woman doesn't kill her," Melanie whispered to Jenna.

Jenna grimaced, obviously not wanting to say anything negative, but her eyes agreed with Melanie.

"Nicole, just let Kay decide, all right?" Leah's thinly arched brows pinched together as if she were getting a headache. "She already said she has a lot to do today."

"And so do you," Kay told her, picking up a makeup sponge and slathering it with foundation. "When you're done with me, one of the hairstylists will work with you. Then you'll need to get your wardrobe assignment and bring down your contest clothes. And you don't want to miss the barbecue tonight."

"Is everyone going to the barbecue?" Jenna asked, raising her voice to be heard. "I mean, it isn't just for guests like the pool party, is it?"

"No. Even the contestants have to eat. The ones who still do, that is," Kay added, with another significant glance at Nicole.

Melanie couldn't help giggling, but Nicole was completely oblivious.

"Leah, do this," she said, pursing her lips and rolling her eyes toward the ceiling.

"Why?" Leah asked testily, clearly not in the mood to comply.

"It'll make it easier for Kay to put on that foundation."

"How is my not being able to see going to help?"

"It's all right," Kay said hurriedly, putting down the sponge and picking up a pencil. "I'll let you know if I need you to do anything in particular. Except hold still, that is. It would make things a lot easier if you didn't talk."

"Definitely, Leah," Nicole reprimanded. "You shouldn't be talking." She smiled ingratiatingly at Kay, as if to say she sympathized with the impossible task she had in putting makeup on Leah.

Melanie watched with increasing disbelief as the session progressed. By the second change of makeup, it was clear that Nicole was driving Leah crazy, but she just kept yammering on, making ridiculous suggestions. Kay seemed to be losing patience as well,

40

her replies becoming more curt as Nicole's questions got longer and dumber. The oddest thing was that Nicole seemed almost desperate to win the makeup woman's favor.

*What does she want?* Melanie wondered. *Free make-up? If so, can't she see she's not exactly making a good impression?*

Apparently she couldn't.

"You know what I like to do?" Nicole asked Kay. "After I get all my eye makeup done, I like to put plain powder over the top, like this." She actually picked up one of Kay's brushes and demonstrated on herself, no doubt staining it green in the process. "I think the mascara lasts longer."

"Hmmm," Kay said, ignoring her.

"You ought to try it," Nicole insisted, lunging toward Leah's face with the same brush.

Kay finally snapped.

"You know what?" she said, snatching the brush from Nicole's hand and slapping it down on the counter. "I've been doing this a few years now. And I must have *some* idea what I'm up to or they wouldn't have hired me. In any event," she added, giving Nicole's face a disdainful once-over, "it's pretty clear I know more about makeup than you do."

Melanie sucked in her breath, waiting for Nicole to react. But once again the girl was Clueless in California.

"Absolutely," she agreed fawningly. "With all the

experience you have? It's a privilege just to watch you."

Melanie and Jenna exchanged incredulous looks. Had Nicole always been so oblivious? Or had a day of smog and sunshine done strange things to her IQ?

*If she keeps up like this*, Melanie thought, sinking a little lower in her chair, *these will be the longest three days of our lives.*

Melanie stuck her head through the open door from the adjoining room. "Do you want to come hang out with us?" she asked Leah. "There's still half an hour before the barbecue starts."

Leah glanced toward the bathroom, where Nicole was taking her third shower of the day. The sound of pounding water was like music to Leah's ears after all that chatter during makeup, then hairstyling, then wardrobe. . . .

"Thanks, Melanie," she said. "But if you guys don't mind, I'd really like a few quiet minutes to myself."

Melanie looked toward the bathroom too and broke into an understanding grin. "Say no more," she giggled, withdrawing her head and closing the door behind her.

Not caring that she was messing up her new hairdo, Leah fell backward onto her bed, exhausted. It felt like midnight, and it was only five o'clock. Worse, in just a few minutes they'd have to go down to the barbecue, and at eight the first event of the actual contest would take place.

*Poise*, Leah thought disgustedly. *What is this, anyway? The fifties?*

Not that she was worried. She knew she had plenty of poise. It just seemed kind of demeaning to be graded on it. *That's one part of the contest I know I could smoke Nicole on, though*, she thought with another glance at the bathroom.

Slowly, almost without her knowing it, her hand stretched toward the telephone on the nightstand. It was two hours later in Missouri. Miguel would probably be home. . . .

*But what would I tell him?* As badly as she wanted to hear his voice, she wasn't ready to answer the inevitable question: Had she made up her mind about marrying him?

Yes, she'd made up her mind. She'd made up her mind the moment he'd asked her. They were too young—to even think about marriage was crazy.

Defeated, she let her hand dangle off the side of the bed.

*I guess I could call Mom again.*

All four girls had telephoned home when they'd arrived at the hotel the night before, but it had been late by then, and no one had talked very long.

*She's probably still at that faculty retreat, though.*

And it wasn't as if Leah had any news she could share with her parents. Despite how close the three of them were, she had no intention of divulging a marriage proposal to her father—he'd probably blow a vein at the mere idea. *Not that Mom would be a lot calmer . . .*

It wouldn't matter that Leah had already ruled out marriage on her own. If her parents even suspected that Miguel was thinking that way, they'd probably ship her off to boarding school in Switzerland. At the very least, they'd forbid her to go anywhere near him. People like the Rosenthals didn't get married at seventeen. They didn't get engaged. They didn't even think about it.

Leah sighed unhappily. *I'll call them tomorrow night.*

# Four

"Now, this is a barbecue!" Nicole pronounced, looking around with deep satisfaction.

Evening had fallen, but the underwater lights in the swimming pool gave the concrete deck a romantic glow, while the portable heaters on their white poles kept the January air warm enough for summer clothing. Numerous white-draped tables had been arranged around the deck, the bud vases in their centers echoing the elaborate tropical flower arrangements floating in the pool. The four girls stood at a table near the grill, finishing their dinners.

"It's a nice party, but you can't really call this barbecue," Melanie objected, picking up a skewer of teriyaki chicken.

"Well, it's a *California* barbecue." Coming from a state famous for its well-seasoned, slow-cooked meats, Nicole knew as well as the next girl what barbecue was. Why couldn't Melanie be more worldly and open-minded?

"I like the fruit," Jenna said, spearing a piece of pineapple. "It's really good."

"It *is* good," Leah agreed.

To Nicole's disgust, Leah had ruined the formal hairdo she'd had done that afternoon by lying around on the bed, and instead of trying to fix it she'd simply removed the pins and combed her hair straight again. Adding insult to injury, most of Kay's red lipstick was now on the wadded napkin in her hand.

"I'm going to get a couple more of those big strawberries," Leah said. "Does anyone else want anything?"

"I'll go!" Nicole offered instantly. "More strawberries coming up."

"That's all right, Nicole. I can get them."

"Don't be silly. It's the least I can do," Nicole said, hurrying on her way, her tall red heels clicking on the concrete.

*Especially with those two judges hanging out over there and all,* she added silently, cranking up her smile as she went.

She wasn't the only one to see the opportunity. At least four contestants were crowding around the table by the time she got there, all feeling the same sudden irresistible urge to eat fruit.

*If Leah was smart, she'd have insisted on coming with me.*

But Leah wasn't taking advantage of any of the million chances to better her odds being thrown her way. Not only hadn't she shown any interest in

Nicole's tips about dressing nicer, she'd barely listened to Kay. And as for what she'd done to her hair . . .

Nicole picked up a salad plate and began loading it with fruit, scooping blindly with her eyes still on the judges. *It should have been me competing this weekend instead of Leah,* she thought for the hundredth time. *That was my contest in Missouri. Why did Leah have to win it?*

Looking down, Nicole suddenly realized she'd taken enough fruit to feed a pig. With a panic-stricken glance at the judges, she hurriedly unloaded half of her overflowing plate back into the display, heart pounding.

The judges continued their conversation.

*It's okay—no one noticed,* she told herself, trying to resume normal breathing. *Everything's cool.*

She sidled closer to the judges, but they still seemed oblivious to her presence. The contestants who had filled their plates before her gave up one by one and went back to their tables, leaving Nicole by herself, hoping for an invitation to join the conversation.

She hesitated, then tossed her freshly washed hair to catch their eyes. Her party outfit was perfect, totally in keeping with the Hawaiian theme, and she'd picked up a makeup trick or two from Kay, even if Leah hadn't.

*She should have paid more attention,* Nicole thought again. *Kay's kind of a grouch, but how many chances do you get to talk to a professional makeup woman?* Watching Kay work had given Nicole the courage to go much more dramatic with her own look.

She cleared her throat—still nothing from the judges. And now there were people trying to get to the table from behind her. Reluctantly Nicole walked on, making sure to keep her chin up and arch her back as she passed the conversing judges.

"Here are your berries," she said distractedly, plopping the plate down in front of Leah.

"Nicole! I asked for a couple! I can't eat this many."

"They're free," Nicole said with a shrug, her eyes on the judges again.

*Oh, no! Now the head judge is over there too! If only I'd waited a couple more minutes.* Chewing her lip, she wondered if she dared risk a trip back so soon.

*I don't know why not. They didn't notice me the first time.*

She took a step in that direction, but Leah stopped her.

"*Now* where are you going?"

"Uh, nowhere," Nicole said, flushing. Maybe it was better to wait a little longer anyway—just in case they *had* noticed her.

Melanie gave her a strange look, then turned to Leah. "What are we doing after the poise contest tonight?"

"I'm going to bed," Leah said decisively.

"At ten o'clock?" Nicole wailed. "You're kidding!"

48

"No, I'm exhausted. Besides, you don't have to go to bed, Nicole. Do whatever you want."

"Like what?"

"The rally might still be going on that late," Jenna said quickly. "You can come check it out with me."

*Oh yeah. That'll happen*, Nicole thought, wondering if Jenna was serious. Who was going to discover her at a Christian youth rally?

"Uh, maybe. What are you going to do, Melanie?" she asked.

Melanie shrugged her shoulders, bare beneath the straps of her white silk dress. "Right now I'm going to get some dessert."

"I'll get it!" Nicole glanced hopefully toward the dessert table. There weren't any judges there, but if she walked past the fruit again on the way . . .

"No, *I'll* get it," Melanie snapped. "By all means, give your feet a rest."

*Now, what's that supposed to mean?* Nicole wondered, watching Melanie stalk off.

*Two more days of this!* Melanie thought as she walked away from the girls' poolside table. *I'm not sure I'm ready for that much Nicole.*

She didn't really want dessert, but she'd have grasped at any excuse to leave at that point, even if only for a couple of minutes. She wound her way through the crowd on the deck, trying to push Nicole from her mind.

U.S. Girls had gone all out on the party, and most of the contestants had dressed as though they were attending a ball at the palace instead of a barbecue at the pool. Not to mention the wannabes like Nicole, who were just as dressed up—or more dressed up—than the contestants. It could have been fun, with someone like Tanya there to giggle about it with, but . . .

Melanie drew a deep breath. She was getting more bored by the minute.

She imagined describing her trip so far to the other cheerleaders back home: "Well, first we went straight to the hotel, and then we pretty much stayed there." Not exactly edge-of-the-seat stuff, not to mention that she could have frozen her butt off beside a pool without ever leaving home.

*At least if Jesse had come, we could have gone driving around*, she thought, remembering the BMW she'd seen in the parking lot that morning.

The thought stopped her dead in her tracks. *Not likely! You and Jesse are over. For crying out loud, get over it.*

Five feet in front of her, the dessert table was laden with fancy cakes and mousses. Melanie looked them over without any appetite as one by one people walked up and made their selections. Each time a dessert was removed, a young, white-coated waiter replaced it with a matching one from his stock behind the display, and it wasn't long before Melanie was watching him with far more interest than the desserts.

Eighteen or nineteen years old, he was deeply tan, with blond hair sun-bleached platinum in streaks around his face. His hands were large and brown, and a thin, braided leather bracelet circled one wrist below his white jacket sleeve. Melanie stood staring until he finally looked up. The sudden widening of his eyes told her he found her pretty interesting too.

"So, what do you recommend?" Melanie asked, stepping up to the edge of the table.

He looked her over appreciatively, making her thankful she'd abandoned her plan to keep wearing jeans until Nicole freaked out completely.

His fine-edged lips pursed slightly. "From where I stand, it *all* looks good."

They both knew they weren't talking about dessert.

Melanie met his gaze without blinking. "It looks just about right from here, too."

He smiled. "What's your name?"

"Melanie."

"I'm Brad." He gestured around the pool with one hand. "So are you going to win this thing, or what?"

It took her a second to realize he meant the U.S. Girls contest. "No, I'm not even entered. I came here with some girlfriends, and one of them is a contestant."

Brad waited for a gray-haired woman to make an apparently agonizing selection of chocolate mousse and leave the table. "Here with your girlfriends, huh? And your boyfriend . . . where is he this weekend?" he asked as he replaced the dessert.

Melanie laughed, feeling some of the tension she'd been carrying for days finally leave her body.

"Subtle," she teased. "Are you always so smooth?"

"Always." Brad broke into a playful smile that showed incredibly white teeth. "To know me is to be amazed by my uncanny, Don Juan–like instincts."

Melanie laughed again. *Finally!* she thought. *A good-looking guy who doesn't believe he's the most impressive thing on the planet.*

"Do you live around here?" she asked.

"Actually, yes. Do you want to see my apartment?"

"Oh, yeah. That's what I want." Melanie rolled her eyes. "I was just getting ready to ask you."

Brad looked a little sheepish. "I had to try. Just think of it as an open offer."

"I'd rather think of it as the off-base babbling of an otherwise nice person."

"Or that," he agreed. "That's a good way to look at it too."

Melanie picked up a sliver of cheesecake. "Well, maybe I'll see you around."

"Why not after I get off work? I can show you the city the way most tourists never see it."

She hesitated, and Brad made a face, reading her mind.

"That crack about my apartment . . . I was *kidding*.

You're perfectly safe with me. Ask my boss." He pointed to a dignified-looking man standing beside the coffee service. "I've been working here nearly a year now, so if I were a psycho killer or something, he'd definitely know it."

"I don't think you're a psycho killer." On the contrary, she thought he was adorable.

"Then meet me tonight."

"I have to go to a poise contest," she said, intensely aware of how ludicrous that sounded. "I probably won't be finished until at least ten o'clock."

Brad grinned, and the skin at the corners of his brown eyes crinkled. "On a Saturday? Things in this town don't even get started till then."

"Hi! How are you?" Jenna shouted into Julie's ear.

The redhead was leaning on the brass railing inside the Empire Room, her back to the doors and her eyes on the chaos below. The lower-level chairs had disappeared, and people packed the open floor, carrying on shouted conversations and dancing in rowdy groups to an onstage band whose music Jenna didn't recognize.

Julie turned her head and her expression clouded. "Do I know you?"

"Well, uh, yeah," Jenna stammered, taken aback. "At least you did this morning. Jenna, remember?"

"Oh, I get it," Julie said. "You're the one who went to the lecture with Julie."

"Uh, yeah." Jenna wasn't sure if she was more shocked by the lack of recognition in the other girl's eyes or the way she was talking about herself in the third person.

"I'm Tabitha. Julie's sister." The redhead paused a moment, searching Jenna's face. "Or didn't she tell you she had a sister?"

"Yes. Yes, she did," Jenna said, recovering slightly. "But she didn't . . . wow. You two are the most identical twins I've ever seen!"

"Scary, isn't it?" Tabitha smiled. "We confuse our mom half the time. Use the necklaces—everyone else does." She lifted a gold charm on a chain around her neck and showed Jenna an ornate *T*.

"Oh, yeah," Jenna said slowly, giving the charm a closer look. "I noticed Julie's, but I guess I didn't pay enough attention." She paused, feeling awkward. "So, uh, where is Julie?"

Tabitha shrugged. "Don't ask me."

"Are you two still fighting?" Jenna asked sympathetically, realizing a split-second too late that she was betraying Julie's confidence by admitting she knew they'd quarreled.

*What's the matter with me?* she wondered. *It's not bad enough that I betrayed my own sister?*

Tabitha didn't look surprised by the revelation, though. "What do you think of this band?"

"I—I don't know," Jenna stammered, grateful but

unprepared for the rapid change of subject. "I don't even know who they are."

Tabitha glanced at her sideways. "No one does. That's why they're up there."

Jenna's face must have stayed blank.

"Amateur night?" Tabitha prompted. "This is one of the groups who'll be competing in the Battle of the Bands tomorrow. Whoever wins opens for Fire & Water on Monday."

"Oh! I can't *wait* to see Fire & Water!" Jenna exclaimed, more determined than ever to juggle her schedule somehow to make that happen. "Are you and Julie going?"

Tabitha nodded noncommittally. "Yeah, that ought to be pretty good."

The band came to the end of its song, announcing its name to moderate applause before it yielded the stage to three new musicians. A noisy shuffling of instruments and sound checks followed.

"Well, the new guys are cuter, if that counts for anything," Tabitha said as the group warmed up.

"Only if they can play."

A minute later the trio exploded into music, quickly erasing any doubts on that score. The lead singer, who was also the guitar player, had the kind of voice that went straight to the heart of the lyrics and twisted them a little. He seemed to speak right to Jenna, almost as if he knew her. Halfway into the song, he even started to look familiar. Jenna was certain his face would stay with her for days.

"They're good!" Tabitha exclaimed, echoing Jenna's thoughts. "That's the best group I've heard so far."

Jenna strained against the railing, wishing she could go below and dance. But Leah's poise contest was starting in just a few minutes, and she had to hurry to meet Melanie and Nicole in the auditorium.

*I'll just stay another second*, she thought. *Not that Leah would probably notice if I wasn't in the audience.*

Immediately she regretted the disloyal impulse. Leah was counting on her.

"I'm going down there," Tabitha said, pointing to the area in front of the stage where a bunch of girls were gathering. "Want to come?"

Jenna glanced reluctantly from the stage to her watch. "Thanks, but my friends are expecting me. I'd better go."

Tabitha nodded and pushed off the railing. "Okay. See you around."

"Say hi to Julie for me."

Before she could change her mind, Jenna turned and hurried from the room, the lyrics of a song she wished she knew pelting her back.

# Five

"More eye shadow!" Nicole insisted, reaching to take the brush from Leah's hand. "Here, let me help you."

"No, thanks." Leah yanked the brush in the opposite direction, not about to let Nicole get a grip on it. "I'm done, anyway."

Putting the brush on the makeup table, Leah kept it pinned under her hand as she rose to her feet, ready for the poise part of the contest.

"Kay used more," Nicole said stubbornly.

"Yeah, but that was for the evening gown thing. Tonight all I really need is lipstick." Leah pointed to her lips, which were painted a full, deep red.

"I still can't believe she didn't have berry," Nicole said worriedly, reaching to rearrange a strand of Leah's hair. "Are you nervous?"

"Not as nervous as you are," Leah teased. "Come on, let's go."

At first she had been leery about letting Nicole come backstage with her—not that she could have stopped her—but now, swallowed up in the pandemonium of fifty girls nearly ready to go onstage, she was actually glad to have her there. Nicole had tried to change nearly every aspect of her plain black outfit, understated makeup, and minimalist hairstyle, of course, but for the first time since they'd arrived in Los Angeles, Leah believed that Nicole was really there to support her. The way she'd fussed over every detail of the preparations, even down to rearranging the fold in the neck of Leah's sweater, reminded Leah of an obsessive young mother sending her precious only child off on the first day of kindergarten. Leah half expected Nicole to spit on a tissue and try to wipe her face with it. Except that that might remove some of the makeup Nicole had lobbied so hard for. . . .

The door to the backstage area was at the end of the long makeup room. A crush of contestants already clustered around it, waiting to be let in. Leah and Nicole joined the jittery group, Nicole as jittery as anyone there. She shifted from foot to foot, looking off balance in her high heels, while her hands rubbed up and down her bare arms.

"Will you relax?" Leah told her. "It's not that big a deal."

A dark-haired girl glanced at them sideways, taking in Nicole and her sleeveless dress in one contemptuous glance. "I'd be nervous too," she said, "if I were going onstage wearing that."

Nicole's mouth dropped open at the unprovoked insult. Her eyes blinked with stunned hurt.

"I'm the one who's competing," Leah said quickly.

The girl's scornful gaze flicked to Leah, then back to Nicole. "That makes a *little* more sense. Beauty may only be skin deep, but hick's all the way to the bone."

"You *need* to dress up, Delia," another contestant said before Nicole could gather her wits. "The judges are interested in brains tonight, so it's obviously to your advantage to distract them if you can. Speaking of which, how much padding is in that push-up bra you're wearing?"

Several girls giggled. Delia's face clouded with rage.

"How much padding's in the seat of your pants?" she shot back. "Because I know your butt can't be that big."

"Oooh!" someone squealed. "Psych!"

"Are you all children?" someone else asked contemptuously. "It shouldn't be hard to stand out for poise in this group."

An immediate silence descended, but the critical once-overs continued until the backstage door finally opened and everyone began filing through it. Most of the girls could barely conceal their impatience, but Nicole hesitated. As soon as Delia had gone on in front of them, she pulled Leah to the side by her sleeve.

"What was that all about?" she whispered shakily,

glancing nervously toward the backstage door. "What did I do to her?"

Leah shook her head. "Nothing. She was just trying to rattle your cage."

"But . . . why?" Nicole's worried expression showed how successful Delia's rattling had been.

"Because it's a *contest*, Nicole. She thought you were in it, and she wanted to throw you off."

"That's not very nice."

Leah stared incredulously. "What did you think? That everyone was going to stand around complimenting each other?"

"No. I'm not that dumb. But . . . well . . . I didn't think it would be like this!"

"There's a lot at stake here, Nicole."

"I know. But still!"

Leah shrugged. "I guess any time something gets this competitive, people's true colors come out. It's kind of hard to take seriously, though." Her eyes flicked around her at the diminishing crowd of hypergorgeous girls. "It's hard to take any of this seriously."

"I take it seriously," Nicole said sincerely. "I take it *very* seriously."

Leah finally saw her chance to say something she'd been thinking a long time. "Maybe you shouldn't. You might be happier."

She could have said more, but the stage manager

came by to hustle the last few stragglers through the door.

*It's probably just as well*, Leah thought, guessing Nicole wouldn't have listened to a lecture anyway.

Besides, with the poise contest about to start any minute, she had a few other things on her mind.

"When is it going to be Leah's turn?" Nicole whispered impatiently as the contestant from Montana rambled on about her recycling plan to save the world. "They ought to do this alphabetically."

Nicole had stayed backstage until the last possible moment, but just before the poise event had begun, she'd hurried into the audience to sit between Jenna and Melanie. Now she sat watching as contestant after contestant was called to the microphone to answer seemingly random questions, everything from "What's the biggest problem facing youth today?" to "What brand of mascara do you use?"

"At the rate this thing is moving," Melanie replied, "I'm starting to wonder if we'll ever see her. Three minutes doesn't *sound* like much . . ."

"Until you multiply it by fifty," Jenna said, checking her watch again.

"Leah's turn has to be coming soon," Nicole murmured, not wanting to admit that, once again, she was finding the events somewhat boring.

*Still, this isn't really modeling*, she reassured herself.

*Real modeling wouldn't have so much waiting around doing nothing.* At least, she hoped it wouldn't.

Not to mention the backbiting. Once they'd figured out she wasn't a contestant, the other girls had left her alone, but that hadn't stopped them from sniping at one another, becoming more and more cutthroat as the time approached when the curtain would rise. Most of them weren't as nasty as Delia, settling for a simple icy stare or contemptuous glance, but even so . . .

*You knew it was a competitive business,* Nicole told herself, her shock already wearing off. *You'll just have to toughen up.*

A burst of applause interrupted her thoughts. The contestant from Montana was finally walking off the stage.

"It is now my pleasure to introduce Ms. Leah Rosenthal," the announcer said into one of the two onstage microphones. "Our U.S. Girl from Missouri."

"Yes!" Nicole exclaimed, sitting bolt upright in her seat to applaud with Melanie and Jenna.

Leah strode out confidently, her long legs bringing her to the contestants' podium in a few sure steps. Her all-black outfit looked sleek and classy against the deep red of the curtain as she raised the microphone and regarded the audience calmly.

"Hello," she said, beginning what Nicole now recognized as a pat introduction speech. "My name is

Leah Rosenthal, and I'm representing the state of Missouri from the town of Clearwater Crossing."

Melanie and Jenna whooped loudly, but Nicole clapped more cautiously, not wanting to prove Delia right by acting like a hick in the big city.

"All right, Leah," the announcer said. "If you had one wish for the whole world, what would it be?"

Leah's eyebrows went up a little at the impossibility of the question. "Well . . . world peace, I guess. I know it's kind of a cliché, but what else would a person wish for under those conditions? You have to have peace before any of the other wishes make sense."

She paused a moment, still thinking. "Unless you wish for love. Because love would imply peace, wouldn't it? So then you'd have both. Maybe that's why Jesus said that loving your neighbor is the second most important commandment. Okay, so maybe it's hokey, but I'm going to change my answer to love."

"I can't believe she said that!" Nicole groaned, horrified. "They're going to think she's some sort of religious fanatic."

Jenna turned to stare at her.

"Well, they are!" Nicole defended herself, refusing to feel guilty. There were times when it was okay to talk about religion and times when it was better to keep quiet. Everyone knew that.

"It's not like she preached a sermon, Nicole,"

Melanie whispered from her other side. "I don't think it's a big deal."

"Whatever." Nicole tried to push down her misgivings. If *Melanie* wasn't put off . . .

"If you could be any animal," the announcer continued, "what animal would you be?"

"You're kidding, right?" Leah's surprised laughter was so genuine that most of the audience laughed along with her. "If I were an animal, the scholarship I'm hoping to win here wouldn't do me much good."

Nicole joined the second wave of laughter that swept the auditorium, relieved that Leah seemed to have won the crowd over despite her rocky start.

"If you discovered that a friend of yours was lying to you, what would you do about it?"

Leah's face became as serious as it had been silly a moment before. "I don't have friends who lie to me. Which is to say that anyone who'd lie to me is no friend of mine. I'd cut them loose. If that sounds harsh, I'm sorry. But I'm an honest person myself, and I expect honesty in others."

Nicole slid down in her seat. It *did* sound harsh. Couldn't she have just said she'd talk to them or something?

"Final question," said the announcer. "What do you think the best thing about high school is?"

Leah was smiling again. "Well, it's definitely not the cafeteria food, so it must be all that relaxing quality time between classes."

More laughter filled the hall.

"No, you really want to know?" she said. "It's my friends. My best friend moved away over the summer, but through a weird set of circumstances I found a great group of new ones this fall. I'm pretty independent, so it's not like I couldn't get through school on my own, but having friends around definitely makes being there more fun. There are eight of us all together—four girls and four guys. The other three girls are sitting right out there."

Leah pointed into the audience, directly at Nicole, then rolled her eyes playfully. "I don't know why, but for some reason my mother thought we should leave the guys at home."

She waved good-bye and left the podium with the audience still laughing.

The announcer allowed only a few seconds for things to simmer down before he called the next contestant. "Introducing Ms. Eileen Capshaw! Our U.S. Girl from Oklahoma."

"So what are we doing tonight?" Nicole asked the others, no longer interested in the contest now that Leah had left the stage.

"We'd better wait and see what Leah wants to do, don't you think?" Jenna replied.

"She still says she's going to bed." Nicole didn't bother to hide her annoyance. "She's dead set on it."

"Then I'm going back to the rally," Jenna said. "Do you guys want to come?"

"Not me," Melanie said quickly. "I've got something to do."

*Sure you do*, thought Nicole, positive Melanie was only making excuses to get out of a Christian rally.

"Okay," Jenna said easily. "How about you, Nicole?"

Instead of answering, Nicole turned to question Melanie. "What are you doing?"

"Just something, all right?" Melanie answered testily. Even if she really had a plan—and how could she?—she obviously wasn't going to invite anyone else to join her.

Meanwhile, Jenna was still staring at Nicole expectantly.

"Well, okay," Nicole said reluctantly, afraid to guess what Courtney would say if she ever found out her best friend had traveled all the way to California only to spend Saturday night at some sort of glorified church camp.

*That's why she's not going to find out*, Nicole promised herself. *Courtney and I have enough problems already.*

"So, is this what you usually do on Saturday night?" Melanie teased Brad. "Cruise Hollywood Boulevard?"

"Not exactly," he said, turning his head to smile at her from behind the steering wheel. "Then again, it's hard enough to find clubs that *I* can sneak into. With you being only sixteen . . . wow. I still can't believe you're that young."

66

*Imagine how surprised you'd be if you knew I was really fifteen*, Melanie thought, wondering what always compelled her to lie about her age to guys. It was like a reflex or something. The only guy she'd ever dated who'd known her real age when they'd started was Jesse, and Jesse—

*Would you forget about Jesse already? You can't even call that dating.*

She turned her head away from Brad, looking out the passenger window as his car stopped in backed-up traffic.

"Pull over!" she cried, hurriedly cranking the window open. There, just ahead, was the famous Chinese Theater, lit up like a power plant. She'd seen so many pictures of the spot, it almost seemed as if she were coming back to a place she'd been to before, except that her heart thudded with the thrill of seeing it in real life. "Could you pull over here?" she repeated. "I want to take a picture."

"Sorry." Brad shook his head. "There's no way to get to the curb in this mess. Take a picture through the window."

Melanie unbuckled her seat belt and scrambled up onto her knees. Leaning far out the window into the cold night air, she snapped away over the roofs of the other stopped cars, hoping at least one of her shots would come out.

"I hope you know you look like a total tourist," Brad said, laughing. "Come on, we have to go now."

A chorus of horns from behind confirmed that cars were moving again.

Melanie dropped back into her seat, flushed with excitement. "I *am* a total tourist," she said happily as Brad drove off. "What's next?"

They had already stopped at the Hard Rock Cafe for a late-night snack, driven by the house Marilyn Monroe died in, and cruised the Sunset Strip, the center of the nighttime action. Melanie couldn't remember the last time she'd had so much fun. Brad was a dream: funny, handsome, easygoing. . . .

"Well, if you're into photography now, we could always drive back down to the end of the Strip and take some pictures of the crew that hangs out by the Roxy. That would jazz up your scrapbook."

Melanie crinkled her nose. "I've seen enough weirdos for one night. How about the beach? I'd love to see the ocean."

"Oh, right! There aren't any weirdos at the beach!" Brad hooted. "Anyway, it's too late for that."

"How come? There's a big moon out tonight, and it's not that cold. Why can't we just walk along the sand?"

"You *are* from a small town, aren't you?" he said with a chuckle. "I'll grant you it sounds romantic, but . . ." He shook his head. "I'd just as soon see my next birthday. I'd love to take you to Venice tomorrow, though. Talk about tourists! You'll fit right in."

"All right. I ought to be getting back to the hotel anyway."

"Already?" In the reflected lights from the street, Brad's blond streaks shone like silver, framing his disappointed face. Shadows hid his eyes, but a bar of light fell across his pouting lips, emphasizing his perfect mouth. He was quite possibly the handsomest guy she'd ever been out with. And here they were, alone together half a country away from home, with no one to check up on them. . . .

Melanie didn't even want to admit to the kinds of thoughts suddenly running through her head. Instead she drew a shaky breath and forced a smile to her lips.

"Sorry, but I don't want to give my friends a heart attack," she said with practiced lightness. "Nicole's already in a snit because I wouldn't tell her where I was going, and Leah's competing again in the morning."

"Your friends don't know where you are?" he asked, clearly startled. "Why not?"

"Because if I'd told them where I was going, they'd have wanted to come with me." *One of them would have, anyway.*

"Oh, I get it," Brad teased, grinning. "And you wanted to keep me all to yourself."

"Sure. If it makes you feel good."

They didn't talk much on the drive back to the hotel. Melanie watched Brad surreptitiously as the intersections ticked by, his attraction—and her resistance to it—growing by the second.

"What's your last name?" she asked suddenly.

"Now you *are* getting serious. It's Howell. How about yours?"

"Andrews."

They were silent again until he pulled up under the hotel canopy and switched off his car engine.

"Well . . . I guess this is good night."

Melanie nodded, one hand already on the door handle.

"I had a lot of fun." He turned in his seat to face her, stopping her in place. "Did you?"

"Um, yeah," she said uncomfortably. She knew what was coming next—and for once she wasn't ready to deal with it. "Thanks. I was going stir-crazy in the hotel."

"Are we on for the beach tomorrow, then?"

Melanie sighed, torn. "If I can get away. I'm not even sure when Leah's contest is over, or if we're supposed to do something after that, or what's supposed to happen."

"But if you're free, you want to go?" Brad persisted.

"Sure."

"Then I'll find out," he said, smiling mysteriously. "I have friends in low places, you know."

"That actually sounds kind of scary."

"Not in this town. There are a lot more low places than high ones."

"Oh." She cracked the door open and began to slide out.

"Can I kiss you good night?"

She had known that was what he wanted, of course. She just hadn't expected him to be so direct.

"Well—uh—I—" she stammered stupidly, embarrassed.

*Why am I acting like such an idiot? One kiss is not a big deal.*

But suddenly it seemed like one. And her hesitancy only grew as she looked for a reason why in Brad's handsome face. Brad was great: sweet, good-looking, available. . . . She ought to *want* to kiss him. So why did she feel almost guilty? Almost as if she were betraying—

*Jesse. Oh, please. Not again!*

Quickly, before she could think another second, Melanie leaned across the gearshift and gave Brad a quick kiss on the lips.

"See you tomorrow," she whispered.

The she let herself out of the car and ran for the hotel.

# Six

The Hearts for God rally was holding its Sunday-morning service on the roof of the hotel tower. Jenna had mistakenly gone down to the Empire Room first, so she arrived late, bursting out of the stairwell and blinking in the sunshine, disoriented by the unfamiliar scene.

One end of the enormous rooftop was filled with row upon row of white folding chairs, arranged like church pews with an aisle down the center. At the front of the aisle, a dais with a white canopy created the effect of a giant outdoor wedding, except that the guests—several hundred teens in matching purple T-shirts—were way too rowdy for a wedding. Four acoustic guitarists on the dais played into four standing microphones, while a woman at a podium in their center led the entire rally in a popular song. The unpracticed voices swelled raggedly, drifting off into the blue sky as Jenna scrambled into an empty seat and read the back of the purple shirt in front of her:

*They must have gotten those today,* she realized, wishing she had one too. The shirts created such a sense of unity that Jenna wanted to be part of the group—not to mention less conspicuous than she suddenly felt in her favorite yellow sweatshirt.

The song came to an end, and the woman at the microphone began a prayer.

"Father, we thank you for this morning, and for the chance to come together today to lift up our hearts to you."

The words were greeted by a raucous cheer. Jenna was so surprised that for a moment she didn't join in.

Then it struck her—why *not* cheer? The weather was perfect, the City of Angels sprawled at their feet like a prize, and no fair person could deny what a blessing it was simply to be young and free. In fact, now that she was thinking about it, it seemed almost ungrateful not to cheer at every church service. She added her voice to the others, throwing in a whistle for good measure.

"We thank you for this opportunity to grow together in faith," the woman continued, "and we offer our spirits and our songs."

When the guitarists started up again with a hymn

that Jenna knew well, she was ready to sing her heart out. She wasn't the only one, either; the rooftop practically burst into sound. And as the song came to its final notes, she knew the unity she'd felt had been created by more than T-shirts.

The woman left the podium, and her place was taken by a youth minister.

"The Bible tells us to trust in the Lord with all our hearts, and not to lean on our own understanding. 'In all your ways acknowledge him, and he will make your paths straight.'" He paused to look around. "That sounds pretty good, doesn't it?"

A murmur of agreement ran through the crowd.

"So why do we so often feel he can't help us with our problems? 'I would turn this over to the Lord,' we say. 'I'd *love* to turn this over. But God can't help me with *this*.' "

Immediately Jenna thought of her situation with Caitlin.

"Can't we all think of something that's not right in our lives?" the minister continued. "Something we'd love to change?"

If she'd only minded her own business, she and Caitlin would still be friends!

"Why not turn that problem over to God this morning? Trust in the Lord with all your heart, the proverb says. Rely on God to make your path straight."

Jenna considered the minister's words. It was awfully tempting to shift her burden onto God, but on the other hand, she could hardly blame God for the predicament she was in. That was the most upsetting part of all: She knew she had no one to blame but herself. The minister had to be talking about problems outside a person's control, she decided. He couldn't be saying that people should just go around messing up, then trusting in God to bail them out.

Could he?

*That wouldn't be right at all. Aren't people responsible for their own mistakes?*

Jenna heaved a tremendous sigh. *I got myself into this mess, and I have to get myself out.*


"I feel like a chalkboard," Leah complained as Kay put the finishing touches on her morning makeup. "Or maybe a paint-by-number."

"You're a work in progress," Kay replied. "There!"

She stepped back to take a final look, then waved her powder brush like a magic wand. "You're perfect. Good luck," she added before she moved off to help someone else.

"Well, this is it." Leah spun slowly around in the makeup chair to face her three waiting friends. By some miracle Nicole had finally been convinced to sit against the opposite wall with Jenna and Melanie, although not before she'd driven Kay nuts with her questions again.

"You look great," Melanie said. "Just do what you did in St. Louis, and I'm sure you'll be fine."

"I don't remember what I did in St. Louis. I barely even remember being onstage."

"You're nervous," Nicole said tensely. "You have to think positive."

"I'm positive I'd rather be doing practically anything else."

"Well, I can't wait," Jenna said. "I'm still kicking myself for missing your big win back home."

Leah tried to smile, but her lips felt numb. In just a few minutes the contestants would gather backstage for the morning event: modeling U.S. Girls jeans. The format was similar to that of the event in St. Louis. Each contestant, wearing a red-white-and-blue outfit, would walk the stage for the judges, showing off her jeans and her personal style. But unlike in St. Louis, the judges wouldn't be picking a winner. The "What Being a U.S. Girl Means to Me" essays would be discussed next, before the evening gown modeling later that night. And that was just to get to the first cut Monday morning, when the field would be narrowed to twenty girls.

"At least we don't have to go to another of those boring formal lunches today," Leah said. "You guys ought to do something fun while I'm in that essay meeting. We can get together afterward and go out to lunch."

She paused a moment, fiddling with the ring dangling inside her shirt. "Of course, if I don't make the cut tomorrow morning, we'll have the whole rest of the day on Monday to go wild."

"You'll make the cut," Melanie predicted confidently.

"I think so too," said Jenna.

"Of course you will!" Nicole said sternly. "For Pete's sake, Leah, stop thinking like that!"

"Now for one last look at all the contestants," the announcer boomed. "Round robin, please, girls."

Rock music filled the room, and all fifty U.S. Girls stepped out from their places against the curtain and began walking to the beat. They filed up one side of the stage, along the front edge, then back toward the curtain again, strutting for the judges as they made loop after loop.

*This is so cool!* Nicole thought, enraptured by the scene in front of her. She was so absorbed that she was barely aware of Jenna, Melanie, or anything else in the auditorium. Each of the contestants had already been announced and had made the circuit individually, and now, with all of them walking at once, it seemed like a Paris fashion show. Leah looked tall and strong, the faint hint of disdain on her face only making her seem like a pro. She'd done well, and Nicole was excited for her.

The music ended, the contestants took a brief, synchronized bow, and everyone filed off the stage.

The audience applauded as the house lights came up, signaling the end of the event.

"That was fantastic!" Nicole exclaimed, clapping enthusiastically. "Now, *that* was modeling!"

Not like that horrible poise contest the night before. No one cared about the answers to those questions—modeling was about being seen, not heard.

"Leah looked terrific," Melanie said.

"Completely," Jenna agreed.

Down at the front of the room, the judges were still busily scribbling on their score sheets. Nicole had been so fixated on them since the day before that she could recognize each one by the back of his or her head now. The chief judge finished first, putting down her pencil, and one by one the others stopped writing as well. The audience was already filing out, but Nicole stayed where she was.

*Why haven't any of them noticed me?* she wondered. It certainly wasn't for lack of trying. She'd used half the clothes in her suitcases the day before, and at breakfast that morning she'd really dressed to wow, in a pink cotton dress and platforms straight out of a forties movie. Despite Melanie's comment about Halloween, Nicole had sailed into breakfast with her head held high. A model had to set herself apart. After all, it was her job to be different and carry it off.

*And I think I carried it off pretty well.*

So why hadn't anything happened?

Nicole's eyes narrowed, as though she could read the backs of the judges' heads for some sort of clue, and for the first time since she'd left Clearwater Crossing, she felt a little jab of fear. The weekend was essentially half over, since for the next two hours the judges were going to be closeted in essay meetings, out of reach and out of sight. Shouldn't one of them have approached her by now?

Melanie and Jenna stood up, ready to leave, and reluctantly Nicole rose too, smoothing the wrinkles from her blue velvet miniskirt as she followed her friends to the exit.

*Maybe I've been too cocky,* she thought. *Just because God gave me this opportunity doesn't mean he doesn't expect me to work for what I want.*

Nicole took a deep, reassuring breath. *Okay. So I'll just have to try a little harder.*

But instead of being scary, the thought brought a smile to her lips.

*Those judges ain't seen nothing yet.*

# Seven

"I can't believe this place. It's packed!"

Melanie was so distracted by the crowd around her that she barely noticed the soda Brad was trying to put in her hand. People jammed the paved board-walk and spilled over onto the wide sand beach, dressed in everything from polar fleece to bikinis to hats straight out of the tea party in *Alice in Wonderland*. Tattoos and piercings were more common than socks.

"This is nothing." Brad punched a straw through the lid of her cold paper cup, almost knocking it right through her fingers. "I guess it's a little more crowded because of the holiday weekend. Plus it's warm—we don't always have this kind of weather in January, you know. But if you really want to see something, you ought to see it on the Fourth of July."

"I'd like to."

Melanie had always been happy living in Mis-souri, had certainly never regretted having been born in the Midwest. But there was something about

Venice Beach she found incredibly magnetic. Not only did she wish she could see it again, she suddenly found herself wondering about all the other famous beaches up and down the coast: Malibu, La Jolla, Big Sur. . . .

"There's a bench," Brad said, pointing to one at the edge of the boardwalk. An elderly couple in matching denim jackets was just standing up to leave. "Quick, grab it before someone else does."

Melanie wove through the pedestrians, skaters, and bicycles between the sidewalk café where Brad had just bought their drinks and the bench on the other side, narrowly avoiding collisions with a guitar-playing skateboarder and a kid wearing Mickey Mouse ears. She and Brad eventually reached the bench in safety, hurriedly spreading out to discourage unwanted company.

"Ah, this is more like it," Brad said, leaning back and stretching his legs out in front of him.

His deep winter tan contrasted with the curly blond hair on his calves and thighs. As Melanie watched, he shucked off his T-shirt, exposing more blond hair curling in a continuous line down his belly to his baggy board shorts. His shoulders were broad and smooth, marked only by a few dark freckles. In a flash she found herself reading his life in those shoulders: summer after summer at the beach with his friends, paddling surfboards until his muscles ached, his skin getting darker, his hair getting lighter, earning his freckles one by one, like badges of West Coast honor. . . .

"Like what you see?" he asked, laughing.

"It's amazing," she replied smoothly, not about to admit she'd been checking him out. "I've never been to the beach before. I've seen it on TV a million times, of course, but it's different to be sitting here in person. It's just so . . . I don't know. Big."

She looked out toward the horizon. The strip of beige sand in front of her ran into a dark blue sea, which in turn joined a bright blue sky. The January sun hung low, warming her bare arms and legs. And in her nostrils the smell of salt air expanded to fill her whole body. She breathed in deeply and finally understood why Jesse was always whining about California.

*Missouri must seem as exotic to him as this place does to me*, she thought. Had Jesse come to Venice, too? For all she knew, he'd sat on this very bench. And did he miss it now?

*He'd have to. A person could get so lost here. Just float off into those stark white clouds and never, ever—*

"I'll tell you what's amazing," Brad offered. "And it isn't the beach."

Melanie snapped back to the present as the flirtatious comment registered. She turned to face him, ready to reciprocate, then stopped abruptly.

She didn't know what to say.

And with a start she realized why. She had half expected Brad to be Jesse. More shockingly, she'd wanted him to be.

The mere idea threw her into a panic.

*No, I don't* want him to be Jesse, she thought immediately. *Am I crazy? Why can't I get it through my head that I broke up with Jesse?*

Especially with Brad sitting inches away. Even a casual observer could see she'd traded up. Brad was everything Jesse wasn't: humble, easygoing, gorgeous. . . .

*All right, they're both kind of gorgeous. That isn't really the point.*

She wasn't actually sure what the point was anymore.


"Are you coming?" Jenna asked for the second time. "I want to hurry and get down there."

Nicole grimaced into the bathroom mirror, out of Jenna's view. "I guess. Just let me touch up my makeup."

"You really don't need any makeup," Jenna said anxiously, sticking her head in from the bedroom.

"Will you stay calm?" Nicole replied irritably, waving her away. "I think I know what I'm doing."

She still couldn't believe Melanie had taken off to the beach with some guy she'd just picked up. What was worse, she hadn't even invited Nicole and Jenna! Not that Jenna would have gone—she was so wrapped up in the rally she'd have passed on a trip to the moon. But with Leah in that stupid essay interview, temporarily tying up all the judges, Nicole was left without a plan.

Sighing, she plucked a tissue from the chrome holder on the wall and ran it over her eyelids, toning down her purple eye shadow. Then she blotted off her lipstick and applied a lighter shade. It killed her to wreck such a good makeup job, but it wasn't as if anyone important was going to see her at the rally. Besides, the rally was probably the one place in L.A. where Nicole didn't want to stand out.

"Are you *sure* you don't want to take the hotel shuttle somewhere?" Nicole called to Jenna out the bathroom door. "Maybe do some shopping?"

Jenna immediately appeared in the doorway again, her round face agitated. "We said we'd do that at lunch. If you want to go somewhere else, then go. But don't keep me standing here waiting if you're not even coming. I could have been there ten minutes ago."

"All right, all right. Keep your sweatshirt on," Nicole said, unable to resist the dig at her friend's attire. Checking her own outfit in the mirror, she wondered if Jenna had even brought any nice clothes. Nicole had exchanged her blue mini for tight black jeans, but she still wore the same black lace top.

*It's not that wild*, she reassured herself. She wouldn't wear it to church, maybe, but anywhere else she wouldn't think twice. Shrugging her slim shoulders, she headed for the door.

*If this shirt shakes things up down there, then they really needed the thrill.*

"Ready?" Jenna asked the moment she saw her. Not waiting for an answer, she charged out the open door into the hall. "I'll get the elevator!"

Nicole sulked silently on the ride down to the lobby. *Maybe I'll luck out and no one will be there again, like last night.*

Jenna had dragged her to the rally after the poise contest, babbling about some band she had seen. But when they'd gotten there, the Empire Room had been deserted except for a few small groups of friends lounging around with their feet up on the chairs. Nicole and Jenna had ended up going back to their rooms and watching cable until Melanie finally came back and revealed that she'd been on a date.

*Melanie's having all the fun*, Nicole thought grumpily, conveniently forgetting that when the judges were around she had less than no interest in leaving the hotel. *That girl always gets everything.*

Down in the Empire Room, the scene was total chaos. People in purple T-shirts were running in all directions, laughing, shouting unintelligible things to each other, and furiously writing stuff down. It was clearly some sort of game, but one that was new to Nicole.

"What's going on?" she shouted to Jenna.

Jenna shook her head, her blue eyes wide. "It looks like some kind of game."

*No kidding, Sherlock*, Nicole thought sullenly.

They were still standing on the fringes, watching and trying to figure out the rules, when two dead-ringer twins careened by, their carrot-red hair streaming out behind them and their faces flushed crimson with excitement. They looked so much like Courtney that they could have been her less cool sisters.

And suddenly Nicole wished with all her heart that Courtney had come with her. What a blast the two of them could have had! Unlike Jenna, Courtney would have appreciated the thrill of being in L.A. She would have insisted on seeing *everything*, not just hanging around the hotel.

"Julie!" Jenna cried, running forward. "Tabitha, hi!"

To Nicole's surprise, both twins spun around. "Hi, Jenna," they said in unison.

"We can't talk right now," one of them apologized, waving a wrinkled sheet of paper as if that explained everything.

"No, wait!" the other one cried. "Where are you from, Jenna?"

Jenna's forehead wrinkled. "Missouri. Why?"

"Missouri!" the one with the paper crowed, writing frantically. "What's your last name?"

"Conrad."

"What's your favorite Bible verse?"

"My favorite? You're kidding! I can't pick one favorite."

"Just pick one you like, then," the girl said hurriedly.

"Well . . . James four, verse eight. 'Come near to God and he will come near to you.'"

"Ooh! Good one!" the other twin cried. "We don't have that one yet." She turned eagerly from Jenna to Nicole. "How about you? Where are you from?"

Nicole only stared. Who *were* these people?

Jenna read her mind. "Oh, sorry. This is a friend from home, Nicole Brewster. Nicole, this is Julie and this is Tabitha." She leaned toward Nicole and lowered her voice. "You can tell by the initials on their chains."

*And God help us if they ever switch them,* Nicole thought, looking from one identical face to the other.

"Well, we can always use a backup," Tabitha said. "What's your favorite Bible verse?"

"Um . . . well . . ." Like she walked around with them all on the tip of her tongue! "Why do you want to know?"

"Because that's the game!" Tabitha explained impatiently. "There are something like eight hundred people from twenty-nine states in this room. We have to find a person from every state, and write down their names and Bible verses to prove we actually met them. Whoever has the most states when the buzzer goes off wins."

"Wins what?" Jenna asked.

"Five hundred dollars."

"Five hundred dollars!" Nicole exclaimed. "Can anybody play?"

Julie and Tabitha exchanged rapid glances. "You can join our team if you want to. Teams can have up to five people each—they just split the money more ways."

"I'll help you," Jenna volunteered immediately. "But you can keep my share of the money."

Julie shrugged. "If we won, we were going to donate it to a homeless shelter anyway."

"Oh, good idea!" said Jenna. "I will too."

They all looked to Nicole.

"Um . . . how about, 'then you will know the truth, and the truth will set you free?' " she blurted out, inspired. They could discuss the money part later.

"John eight, verse thirty-two," Julie said, jotting it down. "I like that one too."

The next thing Nicole knew, the four of them were interviewing anyone they could get to hold still, which wasn't an easy task because everyone else wanted to conduct interviews too, not give them. Worse, they all seemed to be from California. If there were truly twenty-nine states represented at the rally, it seemed most of them must have had only one or two people each. In fact, the majority of people Nicole's group questioned couldn't wait to write down Julie and Tabitha, from Oregon, and finding Jenna and Nicole had everyone psyched. Each time the girls approached a new team there was the very real danger of giving up two states while coming away empty-handed.

"The way to win this thing is to be a five-person team from California," Nicole grumbled, frustrated.

Even so, it was still kind of fun. With the stakes so high and the time so short, everyone was firing off questions with total abandon. A person didn't even have to move around that much; it was actually more efficient to just stand in one place and snag bodies out of the crowd flowing by. After the first fifteen minutes, Nicole's group had spread out near a corner and begun catching people as they came around.

"Where are you from?" Nicole called to a guy in a vintage bowling shirt.

He turned, and Nicole caught her breath. He was cute!

"California. How about you?"

*That figures* she thought, not nearly as annoyed as she knew she ought to be. "Missouri," she replied.

"Missouri!" he exclaimed, rushing over with his paper. But instead of asking the expected questions—name and Bible verse—he just stood there, staring.

"Wow," he said at last. "I didn't know girls from Missouri were so . . . well . . . hot."

Nicole's eyes widened at the unexpected compliment, but she did her best to play it cool. "What *did* you think?" she asked coyly, pressing her lips together to make sure she still had some lipstick on. "That we all wore bonnets and aprons?"

"No. Well, not exactly, anyway." He rolled his eyes. "Kind of stupid, huh? It's just . . . Missouri. I don't even know where that is."

*I wouldn't mind showing you.* Nicole felt her cheeks heat up.

"I guess I, uh, need to get your name and Bible verse," he said, obviously as embarrassed as she was.

"Nicole Brewster. John eight, thirty-two," she said, having memorized the numbers through repetition. She expected her interviewer to come back at her with the text, the way everyone else had done, but instead he smiled sheepishly.

"Uh, could you help me out with that one? Most of the people around here seem to be walking Bibles, but I don't have much memorized."

"It's only because they're all using the same ten or fifteen verses," Nicole told him, offering the excuse she'd concocted to explain her own ignorance. She still hadn't quite figured out why *she* didn't know those ten verses, but instead of pondering that, she recited the one she had chosen so that he could write it down.

"Mick! Come on!" someone yelled. "Let's roll!"

"Will you hang on? I've got Missouri here," Mick called back over his shoulder.

"I'm Mick, by the way," he said, turning back to Nicole. "In case you didn't just figure that out. I, uh, I hope I'll see you around later on."

"Me too." She didn't expect it to happen, but it was nice to be admired.

"How many have you got now?" Jenna asked, rushing over as soon as Mick had gone. "Where was that guy from?"

"California."

Jenna groaned, disappointed.

"But look," Nicole said hurriedly. "I did get Texas, New York, and Hawaii."

"Ooh, Hawaii!" Jenna grabbed her by the arm and dragged her over to the twins. "Hey, Nicole got Hawaii, you guys!"

"Way to go!" Julie cried. "What other states did you get?"

The four went into a huddle, trying to figure out what they already had and what they still needed. Since they didn't know which twenty-nine states were available, they were at a disadvantage in the planning department, but it was still fun to see all the states they had already collected. And to Nicole's surprise, it was also fun to read the Bible verses the other kids had chosen. You could tell a lot about a person by the first verse that popped into their head. . . .

An ear-splitting blast from an air horn cut through the other noises in the Empire Room. The sound was followed by a universal groan as people realized their time was up.

"All right, everyone, here's the drill!" a man called from the stage at the front of the room. In one hand he still held the horn, in the other a microphone. "I'm assuming no one has all twenty-nine states, or they'd have already come up to tell me. Does anyone have twenty-eight?"

"Yeah, right," Tabitha whispered skeptically. Their group had found fourteen.

"Twenty-seven?" he asked, pausing. "Twenty-six? Twenty-five?"

Amazingly, he got a response at twenty-four. Three screaming girls and two guys rushed the stage, waving their list triumphantly.

"Twenty-four! Congratulations!" The man shook each of their hands in turn—no easy feat the way the guys were leaping up and down.

"Let's see, that's a hundred dollars each," the man said. "How will you spend the money?"

One of the girls grabbed the microphone, pulling it out of his hand. "We're going to give it back to Hearts for God, to give a kid a scholarship next year. This is the most fantastic experience! We want someone to come who couldn't afford it this time."

"How cool!" Julie and Jenna said together.

A cheer for the winners filled the auditorium. The

scholarship idea was inspired—a gift from the rally, for the rally—and everyone approved. Nicole herself cheered more and more loudly as the wave of team spirit built. And when she was all shouted out, she looked around her and smiled. Being at the rally was almost like being back home. For a moment, she had felt like her old self again.

*Not that I wasn't myself before*, she corrected herself, disturbed.

The good feeling of a moment before evaporated in confusion. What had made her think something so weird?

"Come on, you guys," Tabitha said eagerly, pointing to the other side of the room. "They're putting out punch and cookies."

"Oh, good," said Jenna. "I'm thirsty."

*Great.* Nicole took a deep breath and let it out slowly as she trailed the others to the calorie-laden refreshment tables. Maybe she could find a diet soda at a vending machine somewhere.

*Or you could just have a cookie and punch, like any normal teenager.*

The idea surprised her so much that for a moment she thought Courtney had climbed into her thoughts somehow. Then she shook her head and smiled.

Could one cookie really kill her?

# Eight

"What a disaster," Leah moaned, falling onto her hotel bed. Her body felt like lead against the too-firm mattress, and the tears she'd been holding back welled up in her tired eyes.

*At least the rooms are empty*, she thought, grateful for that small comfort. Wherever her friends had gone to pass the time while she'd been meeting with the essay judges, they hadn't returned yet.

Leah rubbed the back of one limp hand across her aching forehead. *A total disaster*, she thought again. The room blurred a little more, but somehow she managed to keep her tears from spilling over. She wasn't going to cry about something so stupid, no matter how confused or discouraged she was.

*I just wish I had never come.*

She had thought her essay really clever, by far her strongest asset in a competition where every girl was gorgeous. Unfortunately, the judges hadn't agreed. Forget about appreciating her originality in turning the topic "What Being a U.S. Girl Means to Me" into a feminist rant on patriotism—Leah wasn't even sure they'd fathomed it.

"But . . . didn't you understand?" all three judges on her panel had asked at various times. "U.S. Girls is the name of our *company*. We wanted to know how you feel about representing our *products*."

"Yes, I understood," Leah had answered all three times. "But . . ." *Don't you?* she'd wanted to shout.

She knew she had written a terrific essay, full of wit and irony. Could three separate adults actually be so dense as to believe she'd written it out of stupidity?

*Okay, so it wasn't what they wanted,* she admitted now. *It was* better *than what they wanted!* If U.S. Girls was truly going to send five people to college, didn't intellectual initiative count for anything?

"Apparently not," she muttered bitterly, wondering if she ought to bother competing in the rest of the events. Without the essay to fall back on, did she even have a chance?

The phone on the nightstand rang loudly, jolting her half off the bed. She sat up and glared at it for disturbing her silence. Two more rings sounded before she reluctantly decided to answer, snatching the receiver off the hook.

"Hello?"

"Leah?" Miguel said uncertainly. "Is that you?"

She almost began to cry at the welcome sound of his voice. "Miguel? I can't believe it's *you.*"

Her palm went to press down on the silver ring around her neck, but instead felt the way her heart beat beneath it, so fast she could barely breathe. Why was he calling her now, after they'd agreed to talk when she got back? Was he impatient for her answer? And if so, what was she going to tell him?

"Is something the matter?" he asked. "You don't sound normal."

"What? No, I'm okay. It's just . . . I don't even know what I'm doing here, Miguel."

"What do you mean?"

"I had to meet with three different judges to talk about my essay this—"

"The patriotism thing? I loved that! I'll bet you knocked them dead."

"You loved it?"

She tried to sniff back the tears, but they finally spilled over, and she couldn't keep them out of her voice. "Oh, Miguel. I wish you had been on the panel."

"Leah, are you crying? What's the matter? What happened?"

"The judges *didn't* love it. They hated it, in fact."

"They couldn't have hated it."

"They did! They think I'm too stupid to be a U.S. Girl."

"That's the most ridiculous thing I ever heard. You're imagin—"

"No, I'm not. What are *you* doing?" she asked

abruptly, pointedly changing the subject. She'd wanted sympathy, not an argument.

Miguel didn't speak right away, but when he did, he didn't take the bait. "You really want to win this thing now, don't you?"

"No. I mean, no more than before. Maybe less. If it wasn't for the scholarship—"

"The scholarship. Right."

Was it her imagination, or had his voice grown colder?

"Can we not talk about it?" she begged. "I don't want to talk about this now. I don't want to talk about anything."

"Fine. I'll let you go, then. I shouldn't be calling long-distance anyway."

"No, Miguel! That wasn't what I meant. It's just that I'm tired, and nothing's going right. Can't we talk about you?"

He drew an audible breath. "I really have to go. The phone bill . . ."

"Now you're mad at me."

"No. I'd just rather see you in person, that's all. I love you, Leah."

"I love you too," she said, forcing the words past the lump in her throat.

"I'll see you soon. Bye."

He hung up, leaving her feeling even worse than before. He'd obviously expected his call to be a happy surprise, but all she had done was complain.

And bring up college again, like a total idiot.

Then a new thought turned her tears to sobs. While she'd been whining about college and how tough she thought her life was, Miguel hadn't mentioned marriage once.

He'd proposed in so much haste . . . had he changed his mind already?

"Are you *sure* you have to go?" Brad asked Melanie, pulling his car up to the front of the hotel. "I know a great Mexican restaurant I'd love to take you to. Come on," he wheedled, flashing a winning smile. "I'll bet you don't get Mexican like this in Missouri."

"Maybe not, but I promised my friends I'd eat lunch with them." Melanie checked the gold watch on her wrist. "We stayed at the beach so long I'm already late. I really have to go."

He sighed. "All right. But what about tonight?"

"Can't tonight," she said, opening the door on her side of the car. "Leah's got that evening gown thing, and then there's some fancy party."

"I know," Brad said with a wry grin. "I'm working it."

"So you're busy too," she said, confused.

"I'm not doing anything after that. We could get together then."

"Oh. Well, I'll, uh, have to see what Leah wants to do."

It was the truth, but she couldn't help wondering why it caused her so little pain to say so. Brad was incredibly nice, incredibly cute—shouldn't she be dying to see him again? Instead, she hadn't been dating him twenty-four hours and she was already anxious to cool things off—just as she had been with Jesse.

*That's a stupid comparison,* she argued with herself. *Jesse isn't nearly as sweet as Brad. Not to mention that Jesse has about a million irritating qualities. Like . . . well . . .*

She was drawing a total blank.

*Well, just because I can't think of any right now doesn't mean they don't exist!*

But somehow Jesse's many flaws didn't seem so important anymore. Besides, being with him hadn't been all horrible. There'd been the time he'd driven her to Iowa in a snowstorm, for example, just to see her mother's grave. Or even the very first time he'd been in her house, when he'd helped hang her mother's paintings.

As soon as he'd started getting close, though, she'd wanted him gone. And Brad had simply gotten close faster. Melanie stared at him now, her hand tightening on the door.

*What if the reason we broke up wasn't Jesse?* she thought, feeling the first jolt of panic as she recognized a pattern.

*What if it was me?*

* * *

"Now, this is shopping!" Nicole exclaimed, gesturing to the store windows the girls were walking past on Rodeo Drive. "I can't believe I spent all my clothes money in Clearwater Crossing."

Jenna glanced at the nearest shop window but failed to guess exactly what Nicole found so fascinating. The street was sunny, and the trees were nice, but the storefronts weren't anything special. As far as Jenna could tell, the clothes in Beverly Hills were no better than the ones at home—just three times more expensive and displayed on size one mannequins.

"Do you guys want to get some ice cream or something?" she asked, already bored with window-shopping.

"Not me," Leah mumbled distractedly.

"I couldn't eat another bite!" Nicole declared, rubbing her nonexistent belly. "Those salads were huge."

*Those salads were a bunch of lettuce and half a boiled egg.* Jenna had wanted a burger and fries, but she'd been outvoted by the others, who'd opted for a trendy café with "light" cuisine. *It was light, all right,* Jenna grumbled to herself. *Forget about the hamburger, I think they served me the parsley from the side of the plate.*

"Melanie?" Jenna asked hopefully.

Melanie snapped her head around, startled out of a daydream. "What?"

"Ice cream?" Jenna repeated.

"What about it?" Melanie asked.

"Never mind."

"Oh, look at those cute boots!" Nicole squealed, pointing to the next window.

Leah's gaze flicked in that direction. "You can tell they don't get much snow out here," she said, taking in the pink suede platforms.

"They aren't *winter* boots," Nicole corrected impatiently. "They're to wear with miniskirts."

"Oh."

Leah must have known that, but she didn't bother telling Nicole she'd been joking. "Listen, you guys," she said instead. "I'll go to hair and makeup by myself tonight, all right? It'll be simpler."

"If that's what you want." Melanie sounded a million miles away again.

"Simpler how?" Nicole demanded. "It's not like we get in the way!"

Leah didn't answer.

"There's going to be a Battle of the Bands at the rally tonight," Jenna ventured. "Maybe, if your party ends before it does . . ."

She let the sentence dangle, hoping Leah would take the hint, but Leah wasn't paying attention. She was gazing at a Bentley at the curb as if she didn't really see that, either.

Jenna sighed. The four of them were together only in body. In spirit they had retreated into four separate worlds. Even their conversation was out of sync. Jenna watched her blue sneakers cover the pale squares of concrete, feeling totally discouraged.

She missed Peter. When she and Peter were together, they were really *together*, not like this. She'd never felt so alone with Eight Prime before.

*Even though we're really only Four Prime today.*

"Oh, wow!" Nicole screamed suddenly, turning heads on the wide sidewalk. "You guys, it's Tom Cruise and Nicole Kidman!"

Her right arm shot out in front of her, one trembling finger pointing diagonally down the boulevard toward a couple waiting to cross at a distant light. Jenna caught only the briefest glimpse of a dark-haired man and a strawberry blonde in dark glasses before the pair turned abruptly and headed down the side street.

"Tom Cruise?" Melanie's head jerked up. "Where?"

"There! There!" Nicole shouted, circling her finger wildly through the air before dropping her arm to trap her oversized tote bag against her body. "Come on! Let's get their autographs."

The next thing Jenna knew, all four of them were running down the sidewalk at top speed, maneuvering wildly to avoid colliding with the other Sunday shoppers and tourists.

"I've got my camera!" Melanie cried. "How cool would it be to get a picture of us with Tom and Nicole?"

"Framed-poster-size cool." Leah's long legs gobbled up the distance, setting the pace for them all.

"And we *have* to get a picture or no one will ever believe us."

The foursome stumbled up to the corner diagonally across from the one where the celebrities had been. Melanie punched the button to cross the street, while Nicole jogged in place, completely wired.

"They went that way," Jenna said, craning her neck to see down the side street.

"Hurry, hurry, hurry," Nicole chanted to the traffic light.

Red finally changed to green, and the four of them dashed into the busy intersection.

"What were they wearing?" Leah asked as they sprinted over the asphalt.

"She had on a turquoise coat," Nicole answered, breathing hard, "with black bell-bottoms and sunglasses."

"That shouldn't be too hard to spot," said Melanie.

"I think Tom was wearing a turtleneck," Jenna gasped out as she leapt over the curb at the corner.

Everyone turned immediately and began crossing the second street.

"A black turtleneck," Nicole confirmed.

They reached the second corner and without hesitation dashed down the side street the way the couple had headed.

"They could be in any of these stores now," Melanie said. "What if we lost them?"

"We couldn't have!" said Nicole. "Come on, people, these are movie stars we're talking about. They're not going to shop just *anywhere*. Look for a store with class."

Jenna refrained from mentioning the obvious: *All* the stores in that neighborhood had class. "They might still be outside," she said hopefully.

Only five buildings from the corner, Leah spotted the pair through a picture window.

"Is that them?" she asked excitedly, pointing.

The couple was paying for a purchase, their backs to the street.

"It is! It's them!" Nicole squealed. She tried to finger-comb her tangled blond hair into order. "Now, everyone just be cool," she instructed, looking half frantic herself.

"What are we going to do?" Melanie asked. "We can't just walk in there and accost them."

"No one's going to accost anyone," said Nicole. "We're simply going to—"

But before she could tell them her plan, the couple took their shopping bag from the sales clerk, turned around, and headed directly for the door.

"Here they come!" screamed Nicole, completely unglued.

Melanie raised her camera to her eye, ready to catch the stars exiting. Every muscle in Jenna's body tensed. The door burst open. A flash went off.

Then Leah started laughing.

"I'm sorry," she tried to explain to the startled couple. "It's just that we . . . we . . ." She gave up, laughing uncontrollably.

"We thought you were Tom Cruise and Nicole Kidman," Jenna finished for her.

"I wish!" the woman exclaimed, breaking into astonished laughter. Up close she looked nothing like the movie star.

"Me too," her boyfriend teased. They walked off with their arms around each other, the misunderstanding obviously having made their day.

Leah had never stopped laughing. Now Melanie joined in. The two of them leaned against the storefront, still out of breath from running, nearly screaming with laughter. Their mirth was so infectious that Jenna started laughing too. Even Nicole gave up and joined in.

"I . . . can't . . . believe . . . ," Leah forced out between peals.

"We were running all over town . . . gawking like total tourists!" Melanie gasped.

Jenna had a stitch in her side and her legs ached from pounding the pavement in sneakers. Even so, she couldn't stop laughing. "We should have gotten their picture anyway. We'd have laughed every time we saw it."

"I did!" Melanie screamed. "I was so excited, I pressed the button before I looked."

"Well, you can't blame a girl for trying," Nicole

defended herself between giggles. "You have to admit—it did look like them from a distance."

"How great a distance?" Leah asked, sending them all into fresh fits of laughter.

As if they'd agreed beforehand, they all plopped down right there on the sidewalk, still in hysterics, ignoring the sideways glances from curious passersby. Even fastidious Nicole sat on the concrete, ignoring the dust coating her black jeans.

They were winded, laughed out, and more than a little embarrassed before they rose to their feet, but the way they all stood up at once made Jenna's spirit soar.

They weren't just four separate people hanging out anymore—they were a group again.

# Nine

"Line up, girls," the stage manager shouted, hustling through the backstage area and clapping her hands as she went. "Two minutes!"

There was a bustle of frantic energy from the other contestants, all of whom were essentially already in line. They fidgeted in their evening gowns, checking their hair and makeup with nervous hands. But Leah stood twisting the silver ring on her thumb as if she hadn't even heard.

*I wish you were here*, she thought, also wishing the ring could somehow pass that message along to Miguel.

When she'd realized that her strapless dress left her no way to hide Miguel's ring under her clothes, she'd reluctantly untied its ribbon. But its absence had made her feel even more undressed than her plunging neckline. She'd hesitated only a moment before she'd placed the ring on her thumb instead. It looked strangely at home there, despite the formality of her evening gown.

*They want personal style? I'll give them personal style*, she thought, beyond caring about the judges'

107

opinion of a conspicuous thumb ring after their essay-bashing that morning.

"Here we go!" the manager called. "Look sharp, look sharp!"

Music blared through the speaker system, sending the behind-the-scenes tension up another notch. The girls were in line to come out and model their dresses one by one, the way they had done with their jeans that morning. But whereas Leah had been one of the last onstage in the jeans competition, she'd be one of the first this time.

"This is it," the girl in front of Leah whispered to the girl in front of her.

"Yep."

Leah noticed that no one wished anyone good luck.

And then, almost before she knew it, it was her turn. She plunged onto the stage even as some coldly observant part of her brain realized that an abrupt, even contemptuous, entrance was fast becoming her trademark. Then the floodlights dazzled her eyes, and she shut off as much of her brain as she could, concentrating on nothing more than walking and holding her head up high.

The lighting was more dramatic than it had been for the earlier events, making it impossible to spot individual faces in the audience. Leah walked along the edge of the stage, doing her best to show to advantage the expensive dress her mother had bought her. At the very center, where the edge of the stage came closest to the judges, she stopped and struck a few poses to let them see every angle. Her dark green gown clung to her legs, accentuating her height and leanness, sparkling like an emerald where the stage lights caught its sequins. The few loose curls hanging free from her French twist brushed back and forth over her bare shoulders as she posed, tickling more than the touch of glitter Kay had placed there earlier.

*I can't believe I'm actually trying,* she thought, feeling like a fraud as she made turn after turn for the judges.

But at least she didn't have to keep the disdain off her face. She'd learned back in St. Louis that the officials weren't able to differentiate real emotions from contest attitude.

*I'd like to show them attitude,* Leah thought, putting more of it into her step as she walked to the back of the stage to wait out the other girls.

Nicole was already halfway out of her seat in the audience when Melanie caught her by the elbow.

"Where are you going?" Melanie whispered, glancing meaningfully toward the stage. "It isn't over yet."

"I need to use the ladies' room," Nicole lied smoothly. "I want to be ready to beat the crowd."

Leah had modeled long before, and the evening gown contest was sure to end any minute. Melanie glanced at the stage one last time, then let go of Nicole's arm.

"I'll meet you at the party," Nicole whispered, climbing over Jenna's knees on her way to the side aisle.

The other people whose legs Nicole had to climb over weren't quite as nice about it, but she persevered, determined to put her plan into action. And with the evening gown contest almost over, her moment was approaching fast.

*God helps those who help themselves*, she thought as she cleared the last coat-covered pair of knees and stumbled into the carpeted aisle. She leaned against the textured wallpaper a moment, composing herself in the darkness as the final contestant took the stage wearing a red-white-and-blue spangled number.

Nicole's penciled eyebrows rose to the limit. *She looks like a float in a Fourth of July parade!*

And while Nicole could appreciate the I'm-a-team-player message the girl was trying to send, she was shocked that the poor thing couldn't see how overdone she was.

*Leah looked so much better.* Her friend had oozed class compared to the misguided creature at center stage now.

Then the round robin began, with all fifty girls making two more circuits to give the judges their last look. Nicole watched only a second before she began easing down the aisle toward the stage, moving slowly to avoid attracting attention.

Her plan required perfect timing. If she acted too early, she ran the risk of being thought rude, or worse, not being noticed at all. Too late, and she'd be lost in the crowd. If she was going to make this thing work, she had to be in just the right place when the house lights came up.

Reaching the front of the auditorium, Nicole stopped adjacent to the second row and nervously checked the scene. The entire first row had been reserved for the judges, even though they were only using the center eight seats. The seats directly behind them were vacant as well, to ensure their privacy. Nicole's eyes never left their profiles as she made nervous final adjustments to her outfit.

Ever since she'd learned about the big party that night, she'd known what she would wear: the slinky red dress she'd bought for the homecoming formal. After Jesse had taken Vanessa Winters to the dance instead of her, Nicole had almost returned it, certain she could never enjoy wearing anything with such awful associations. But she'd tried it on again before she'd left for the store, and that had been her downfall. A great dress was a great dress—with or without Jesse.

She tossed her head, refusing to think about old crushes on the verge of her new life. The motion barely disturbed her curls, which she had sculpted into a tousled pile, then sprayed so heavily with extra-hold lacquer that not a strand dared leave its place. She put a careful hand to them anyway, then checked her jewelry again.

From the crystal tiara that anchored her curls to her crystal drop earrings and necklace, everything was in place. Wide crystal bracelets cuffed both wrists, lending an elegant touch, and at the hem of her red silk gown, high-heeled silver sandals peeked out to complete her look. Her statement was bold, but Nicole knew she looked amazing because she'd been turning heads all evening. Between her outfit and the makeup tricks she'd learned from Kay—jazzed up with her own special spin, of course—this was truly her night to shine. Just as soon as the house lights came up . . .

The contestants began filing off to one side of the stage. The audience applauded. Nicole put her hands together too, in case anyone was watching her, but quietly, so as not to attract attention. The last girl left the stage. The stage lights went off. The music grew softer.

Nicole tensed, ready.

And then the house lights began to rise. She waited only long enough for them to reach full power before she pushed off from her hiding place.

Between the edge of the stage and the first row of seats, where the judges sat scribbling their final thoughts, was a wide aisle. It was along this aisle that Nicole directed her steps, her head held high, her walk as sexy as she could make it. The rest of the audience was starting to leave its seats, headed for the exits, but Nicole had been the first to rise and now she had the front aisle to herself, exactly the way she had planned.

She walked its length slowly, using every inch. All eight judges were gathered at its center, facing forward, waiting to be wowed. And she was just the girl to wow them.

The first judge looked up as she walked by. Nicole caught the movement from the corner of her eye but didn't turn her head. She did slow her steps slightly, though, prolonging the moment, giving the other judges time. . . .

It seemed only a breathless second later that she had passed them by. Keeping her pace slow and easy, she crossed the room and left through a door on the other side. The rest rooms were in that direction—anyone who didn't know better would assume she was simply on her way to use the facilities. But when the door swung shut behind her, Nicole didn't keep walking down the hall. Instead, she slumped against the wall a few feet away, dizzy with triumph.

Her plan had gone off without a hitch! No one had gotten in her way or blocked the judges' view of her. Her walk had been brilliant, without any slip or awkwardness. And the judges had noticed—she was sure they had!

Reining in her excitement, she set off toward the rest room after all, a radiant smile on her face.

*It can't hurt to touch up my makeup before the party*, she thought, patting the tiny beaded bag hanging from her shoulder.

After all, she wanted to be at her best when the judges came looking for her.

"Well, I'm already bored," Melanie told Jenna, casting a restless glance around the chandelier-lit Westside Room.

The room was larger and fancier than the one U.S. Girls had used for its other banquets, and the dining tables stood off to one side. The china and crystal they'd been set with sparkled in the low light, beckoning to the guests still sipping their drinks and mingling. The room was different, but Melanie noted that the crowd inside was starting to look eerily familiar, although they were all overdressed for the occasion.

*Overdressed being a relative term*, of course, she thought, with a sideways glance at Princess Nicole. Her Royal Highness was over by the juice bar with Leah, chatting up one of the male judges. Melanie had thought she'd already seen it all as far as Nicole's wardrobe went, but she had to admit she hadn't been ready for a tiara. *What is that girl thinking?*

"I wish Leah would get free," Jenna replied, following Melanie's gaze.

For the past fifteen minutes, Leah had been stuck in a conversation that Nicole's constant interruptions had done nothing to cut short. Melanie and Jenna had gradually wandered off to give Leah some privacy, but that idea had apparently never occurred to Nicole, who was soaking up the attention as if the poor man were interested in her instead of in Leah.

"If Leah tries to walk away from that judge, I think she'll have to drag Nicole," Melanie muttered.

"Hors d'oeuvre, miss?" a smooth voice asked at her ear, startling her into spinning around.

Brad was making a silly bow over a silver tray, offering her a pristine selection of pastry puffs.

"I'll take one," said Jenna, taking two.

Melanie was just about to introduce them when Leah and Nicole finally made their way over.

"Food at last!" Leah said, helping herself to two hors d'oeuvres as well. "Whatever happened to dinner?"

"Soon," Brad promised.

"Everyone, this is Brad," Melanie said. "The guy I told you about."

"He's a *waiter?*" Nicole blurted out, sounding horrified.

Melanie stared at her, temporarily speechless, but Brad only smiled.

"Very glamorous, I know. Do you want my autograph?"

115

Melanie burst into surprised laughter at Brad's lucky hit. "If you only knew!"

Nicole looked back and forth from Melanie to Brad as Leah and Jenna laughed too. "No way," she said slowly, confused. "This isn't the *same* waiter. Right?"

"I don't know," Melanie teased. "Don't you think he looks like Matt Damon?"

Nicole smiled slightly, then turned away, not enjoying the joke. "This is the best party ever!" she gushed in an obvious attempt to change the subject. "Isn't it, Leah?"

Leah shrugged. "That depends. If they feed us steak and lobster I might forgive them for boring me to tears. Otherwise, I think I've had more fun at the dentist."

*"Leah!"* Nicole looked quickly around to make sure no one else was listening.

Brad laughed. "Sorry to disappoint you. You're getting chicken and rice pilaf."

"Whoopee," said Leah, making circles with one index finger.

"Waiter!" an impatient voice called.

Melanie looked over to see a woman waving to catch Brad's attention.

"Could we have some hors d'oeuvres over here, please?" the woman asked snappishly.

"Of course." Brad skipped over and handed the astonished woman the entire tray. He was back in an instant, whispering in Melanie's ear. "So what are you doing after this? Do you know yet?"

"No." Melanie didn't bother to whisper in return. "I don't think we have plans yet."

Jenna perked up. "There's a Battle of the Bands in the Empire Room," she said. "Everyone's going to be dancing."

"Oh, yeah. The Christian thing," Brad said, nodding. "But don't you have to be part of the rally to get into that?"

"I have guest passes," Jenna said.

"That works. And I'll get in because I'm an employee of the hotel—who'd better get busy if he wants to keep his job." Brad winked at Melanie. "See you there."

"Brad, wait!" Melanie called to his back, but he didn't hear her over the crowd. She wanted to shout again, more loudly, but there were so many people in the room, she was afraid of causing a scene.

*Great*, she thought, watching him disappear out a side door. Now she'd have to try to catch him serving dinner and change the plan.

"He, uh, he doesn't think we're *all* going to the rally, right?" Nicole asked anxiously. "Because I'm staying at the party with Leah."

Leah raised an eyebrow. "Who said I'm staying at the party? Let's leave as soon as they feed us."

"Really?" Jenna said, lighting up. "You really want to go?"

"I don't see why not. Dancing sounds fun. Besides, if you and Melanie are going, I'd rather go than stay here."

"I didn't say I was going," Melanie put in quickly.

"Me either," said Nicole.

"Why not?" Jenna wailed.

Melanie tried not to make a face. Did she still need to explain after all this time?

"It's just . . . well, you know. That kind of thing isn't for me."

"You don't like dancing?" Leah asked skeptically.

"You know it isn't just dancing," Melanie defended herself. She didn't want to offend Jenna, but there was no way she was spending an evening getting grilled by a bunch of gung-ho Christians.

"No, it is!" Jenna insisted. "It *is* just dancing. Come on, Melanie. Please?"

She looked so hopeful that Melanie hated to disappoint her. "Well . . . all right." Going was easier anyway, and if it turned out to be horrible, she and Brad could always leave.

"No way!" cried Nicole. "If you guys all go to the rally, what am I supposed to do?"

"Gee, I don't know. Come with us?" Leah said.

"And leave this great party?" Nicole whined. "Are you crazy?"

118

Leah shrugged. "So stay, then."

"By *myself?*"

"Would that be wrong?"

"Well . . . *yeah.*"

Leah smiled a little as she shrugged a second time. "So then I guess it's settled. We're all going to the rally."

# Ten

"Isn't this fun?" Jenna shouted to Nicole over the music. She was so excited to be at the Battle of the Bands, she thought some of the thrill might have rubbed off. A moment later, though, she found out she'd been hoping in vain.

"This band isn't very good," Nicole sniffed, rubbing her bare arms. She'd put most of her jewelry in Melanie's purse, but she hadn't wanted to change her long dress.

"Who cares?" Leah was still wearing her formal, too, but whereas Nicole looked stiff and out of place in red silk, Leah somehow managed to blend in in sequins. "It's nice just to be where no one's watching me. Besides, so what if the band isn't great? They aren't bad, either."

"That's right," Jenna agreed quickly, glad Leah had said so first. "I mean, come on, Nicole. These aren't professionals. They're just friends and garage bands, having a good time."

Nicole rolled her eyes. "Whatever."

The Empire Room had been darkened for the big

event, and the folding chairs were gone again. The place was packed, with the majority of the crowd down below, dancing in the colored lights flashing from the stage. Jenna looked around for Melanie, but she and Brad had headed for the dark fringes of the room the moment he'd arrived, and now Jenna wasn't even sure her friend was still in the hotel. She leaned harder against the brass railing, gazing longingly down at the dance floor.

*If only Peter were here*, she thought. And she wasn't missing him simply because she wanted a dance partner. She wanted to share the rally with someone who could appreciate it the way she did. Someone she didn't have to keep explaining or apologizing to. Someone like Peter.

*Or Caitlin*. Jenna sighed. What was almost worse than being in a fight with her sister was not being able to talk to anyone about it. Jenna looked over at Leah and considered confiding in her. She was sure Leah would never repeat one word of anything she was asked to keep secret.

*Unlike me*, Jenna thought unhappily, realizing she would have to keep her problem to herself. How could she talk to Leah without betraying Caitlin a second time?

"I'm going to the ladies' room," Jenna announced abruptly. As eager as she'd been to get back to the rally, suddenly all she wanted was a couple of minutes alone.

"Look for us on the dance floor when you get back," Leah told her, starting to move toward the stairs. "I feel like working up a sweat."

"Who are we supposed to dance with?" Nicole demanded.

"What's the problem?" Leah teased. "I'm not good enough for you?"

The two of them set off, Nicole still grumbling that she wasn't going to dance unless someone acceptable asked her. Jenna turned and walked in the opposite direction, headed for the rest room down the hall.

To her surprise, the place was deserted. *There must be another one off the lower level somewhere*, she thought, taking her pick of empty stalls. It wasn't until she came out to use the sink that she discovered she wasn't alone.

A woman in her twenties was splashing her face at one end of the counter, spattering the mirror with stray drops of water. Jenna hesitated a moment, then took the sink at the other end.

*What is she doing?* she wondered as she washed her hands. *I hope she hasn't been crying.* But why else would anyone wash her face in such a public place?

Jenna snuck another peek. The woman's face was down in her hands again. All Jenna could see clearly was a thick mane of shiny black hair spilling forward over ivory cheeks, so she studied the woman's clothes instead: snug faded jeans, chunky black boots, and a

122

short, fringed leather jacket. Jenna was still checking her out when the woman suddenly dropped her
hands, grabbed blindly for a paper towel, and pressed
it to her face.

"Whew!" she said, wadding the wet white paper
into a ball and dropping it through a slot in the
counter. "If I'd known I was going to be dancing, I'd
have left my jacket in the room."

Her brown eyes glittered behind straight black
lashes as she smiled at Jenna in the mirror. She was
a total stranger . . . and yet she seemed strangely
familiar.

"Have you been in there?" she asked, jerking
her head toward the rally. Her black hair swung
with the motion. "Some of those bands are pretty
good."

Jenna nodded, trying to shake off her weird déjà
vu. "I wasn't there long enough to dance, but I'm going back. Are you?"

"Can't. I've got to meet some people." The woman
headed for the exit. "Have fun."

Her right hand was pushing the door open when
Jenna noticed the unusual set of rings she wore.

"It's you!" she said with a gasp. "You're Kei from
Fire & Water!"

The woman froze, then slowly dropped her hand
and turned around. "I don't get recognized very
often," she said with a sheepish grin. "It still feels kind
of weird."

"Are you kidding? I'm embarrassed it took me so long. I *love* your band!"

"Thanks."

They stood staring at each other.

"Well," Kei said. "I guess I'll be—"

"No, wait," Jenna begged. "I just . . ." She didn't know what she wanted, but she couldn't let Kei go so quickly. "Can I have your autograph?"

"All right. What do you want me to sign?"

"I don't have anything with me," Jenna realized, groaning. "I don't even have a pen! I wish I'd known I was going to meet you. I'd have brought down the T-shirts I bought."

Kei dug in her jacket pocket. "I have a pen," she said, producing a black marker. "But as far as paper goes . . ."

Jenna grabbed a paper towel from the holder and smoothed it out on a dry area of the counter. "I wish it were something better," she said, "but at least it's white."

"At least it's not toilet paper," Kei joked as she scrawled her name across it. "All right, I've got to go. It was nice meeting you."

Jenna was so entranced with her autograph that she barely noticed when Kei slipped out the door. Holding the paper carefully by the edges, she lifted her prize to the light.

*Kei Kulani*

Matthew 19:26

" 'With God all things are possible,' " Jenna said under her breath.

Even though she'd known the verse forever, seeing it there—in such an unexpected place from a person she'd never hoped to meet—made her believe it like never before.

"All things *are* possible," she whispered.

And that was when she knew that somehow, some way, everything would be all right between her and Caitlin. Maybe the damage wouldn't be easy to fix, and maybe it wouldn't happen right away. But it *would* happen.

All she had to do was believe.

"Come on, everyone!" a band member called to the crowd from a microphone onstage. "Put your hands in the air!"

Leah smiled and waved her bare arms overhead, not in the least disturbed that she was dancing alone. Nicole had found a partner, but a lot of other people were dancing singly or in groups, and Leah preferred to be on her own. All she wanted to do was dance the fear, self-doubt, and anxiety of the past few days completely out of her system. The fact that she was getting her contest gown sweaty in the process was of no concern at all.

The song was coming to an end when Jenna ran up and grabbed her by the elbow, her eyes wide with excitement.

"Guess who I just saw?" she demanded. "You'll never guess."

Before Leah could even consider the possibilities, Jenna blurted out her answer. "Kei Kulani! What do you think of that?"

"Uh, maybe if I knew who that was . . ."

"She's the drummer for Fire & Water! And she gave me her autograph! I took it upstairs to keep it safe."

Leah could feel the blank look on her face. She *wanted* to know what Jenna was talking about. She just didn't.

"Fire & Water," Jenna repeated, a little desperately. "You've never heard of them?"

"No, but I really hope Nicole has!" Leah said, laughing. "After all her celebrity hunting, she'll die when she finds out you bagged one without her."

Jenna smiled, but she didn't seem to find the situation nearly as amusing as Leah did. In fact, she looked downright worried.

"What's the matter?" Leah asked. "Is something wrong?"

"It's just . . . well . . . Fire & Water is my favorite band, and they're playing here Monday night. I know you have the finals that night, though, and I probably never should have bought us all tickets in the first place, but I have them now and—"

"Wait. Hold up," Leah interrupted. "You bought

126

four concert tickets and you didn't even mention it? How much did they cost?"

The band onstage started playing again, forcing Jenna to shout her answer. "Don't worry about that. I just thought if things worked out . . . like maybe the times would overlap or something, so we could still see most of the concert." She shrugged. "Otherwise, I'll sell the tickets."

"Don't be crazy! If they're your favorite band, you should go. In the unlikely event that I win, you can congratulate me after the concert."

Jenna shook her head stubbornly. "If you can't go, then I won't either. I wasn't even going to mention it until I knew if it'd work out. But then I saw Kei and got all excited and . . . never mind. We'll just have to see how it goes."

Leah wanted to argue that there was nothing to see, but she had to admit she was touched. Jenna was so obviously dying to go to the concert that it was amazing she'd kept it a secret as long as she had.

"Well, if I don't make the cut tomorrow morning, we'll all go," Leah said. "It'll be fun."

In fact, there was no doubt in her mind that it would be a lot more fun than competing.

But there was also no denying that her pride would be hurt now if she didn't finish in the top twenty. After everything she'd been through, it would be humiliating not to make the cut. Besides she'd come there to win a scholarship, and that was still her goal.

Wasn't it?

"This is our last song," the guitar player announced. "So if you like us, let the judges know by dancing."

"Whatever," Nicole mumbled, launching her body into the number. She'd lost track of how many bands she had already danced to, and she was way past caring about partners. Why go to the trouble of lining up a guy for every song when all around her people were dancing by themselves or in loose, haphazard groups? Leah and Jenna didn't have partners either. They danced on either side of her, the three of them part of the crush of people that had gradually pressed forward nearly to the edge of the stage.

"These guys aren't as good as the girls before them were," Jenna shouted apologetically, as if Nicole were keeping score.

"They're okay," said Nicole.

She wasn't about to admit it to Jenna, but most of the bands had turned out to be pretty good. Any way she looked at it, though, an amateur Battle of the Bands was no substitute for the glamorous party they'd left behind. Nicole wondered if it was over now, and whether the judge she and Leah had talked to had looked for her after dinner. She imagined how things *might* have been—returning to her hotel room, hair and makeup still intact, high on the thrill of her very first modeling contract. Instead she was hot, sweaty, and disheveled, half lost in the crowd at a rally she'd never wanted to go to.

*It isn't fair*, she thought, discouraged. If she was so destined to be discovered that weekend, why was everything conspiring against her? Not to mention how long it was taking! She'd expected something to happen well before Sunday night, and now it seemed she'd have to wait until Monday.

The band onstage closed its final song with a crash of electric guitar chords.

"Thank you!" the lead singer cried, punching the air with one fist. The other members of the band began unplugging their instruments from the amplifiers, even as two new guys hurried out and began plugging in.

The spotlight that had been trained on the band switched to a microphone on one side of the stage as the new group readied itself. A man came up to address the crowd.

"Weren't they great?" he asked. "How about a hand for these guys?"

The crowd was already clapping.

"And now I'd like to introduce the last band of the night. Everyone, please welcome Trinity!"

The spotlight snapped to the new band, and the crowd exploded.

"Oh, these guys are great!" Jenna shouted. "I heard them yesterday."

Nicole reluctantly gave the new group her attention, glad it was the last. The third and final member, the lead singer, had just come out and plugged in his guitar. As she watched, he turned and walked to the front microphone, prompting screams from some of the girls. The unexpected commotion made Nicole look harder as the guy hit a few warm-up chords. His head bent over his guitar, leaving his face half in shadow, but from what she could see he was cute but not that cute. Certainly not screaming-from-the-crowd cute. Pretty average-looking, actually. His hair was reddish brown; his nose was Roman. If Nicole had been in Clearwater Crossing, she'd have thought he looked a lot like . . .

*It can't be,* she thought, doing a shocked double take. *Right? No. How could it? Oh, dear God, I think it is. It is!*

Trinity's lead singer was Guy Vaughn.

"Wait till you hear this guy sing," Jenna told Nicole excitedly. "This band is fantastic."

Nicole just stared. What was Guy Vaughn doing in California? How did he get there? Why?

And then he started singing, and she forgot all her questions.

His singing voice was deeper than his speaking one, but far from sounding as if he had forced it lower, it seemed he had simply relaxed it. Singing, he sounded so real, so sincere—far more so than he'd ever sounded in conversation. *Not that the two of us ever had a particularly real conversation.*

Still, he seemed different onstage. She watched him, stunned into silence. With a guitar in his hands he seemed almost, well . . . cool.

"That guy is so hot!" one of the girls in front of Nicole squealed to her friend.

"Totally cute," her friend sighed back. "I'd give anything to meet him!"

Nicole could barely believe her ears. This was *Guy* they were talking about!

"I went out with him," she blurted.

"You did?" four voices gasped at once.

The two girls in front of her were mesmerized, and Leah and Jenna were staring as well.

"*When* did you go out with him?" Leah asked.

"How?" Jenna put in excitedly.

Nicole shrugged. "A while ago. He lives in Clearwater Crossing."

"You're kidding!" Jenna cried.

"Where's Clearwater Crossing?" the other girls asked.

"Missouri," Nicole answered uncomfortably, wishing she'd never mentioned it. Other heads were turning now.

"What's he like?" one of the strangers demanded. "Tell us everything!"

"Well, there's not a lot to tell . . ."

But everyone was looking at her so expectantly, she felt as if she had to come up with *something*. "I mean, we went to a movie. It was pretty fun."

Her blind date with Guy had actually been a disaster, but no one else needed to know that. Just like they didn't need to know it had been a double date with Courtney and Jeff, or that Nicole and Courtney had horsed around the entire evening like children. Her cheeks burned now at the recollection.

"What movie did you see?" Jenna asked, fascinated.

Nicole squirmed under the intensely interested gazes of four sets of eyes. "It was, uh . . . you know. One of those romantic comedies."

There was no way on earth she was going to admit they'd seen *Too Many Puppies*, a G-rated cartoon. Or that he'd taken her directly home afterward. Or that he'd later told Jeff he never wanted to see her again.

"What's he like?" one of the girls asked. "Is he totally dreamy?"

"Dreamy?" Nicole repeated, barely able to believe her ears. *Maybe to people who use words like* dreamy. *Maybe to a couple of totally sheltered girls at a Christian youth rally Guy would seem pretty dreamy.*

But only because they had no idea what he was really like.

Her eyes went back to the stage. Guy was singing like a pro, his fingers sure on the guitar strings, and suddenly Nicole remembered he'd been about to play guitar the very last time she'd seen him, at the farewell party for Teen Extreme. She'd been so eager to end her exile in Bible class that she hadn't stuck around to listen, but she remembered being sure he'd bore the group with "Kumbaya" or something equally awful.

She wondered what she had missed that day, because the song he was singing now was far from awful. His words seemed to sink right down to her bones, and for the first time since she'd met him, Nicole truly understood how much her immature behavior might have cost her. If she hadn't been so quick to judge, if she hadn't acted more like Courtney's date than his, if she'd taken the time to find out anything about him . . .

So what if all the gaga girls around her didn't have a clue what Guy was like? At least they had an excuse. But Nicole hadn't just been out with him, they'd spent an entire week together in Bible class. And now she had to admit that the person onstage was a stranger to her. Every word he sang only made that clearer.

The truth was Nicole had no idea what Guy was like either. And she'd lost the chance to find out.

# Eleven

"I can't believe this is already our last day!" Melanie said, stirring cream into her coffee Monday morning. She normally didn't touch coffee, but she and Brad had been out late the night before.

"It seems like it just flew by," Jenna said. "Are you nervous, Leah?"

Leah shrugged. "A little. More than before, anyway."

"Of course she's nervous!" Nicole put in. "This is the final cut!"

The girls were eating breakfast in the hotel restaurant before Leah went off to makeup for what could be the last time. All fifty contestants were to assemble onstage that morning to learn who had made the final cut of twenty, from which the five winners would be chosen.

"You'll make it," Melanie predicted, reaching for the sugar. "If you don't, I'll be amazed."

Leah pushed her barely touched breakfast away. "If I don't, at least we'll have the rest of the day to run wild. And we can go to Jenna's concert."

"Will you stop talking that way?" Nicole said.

Melanie wasn't sure if Nicole was delivering another of her pep talks, or if that was her way of saying she wanted to go to the evening's finals no matter what.

"Well, I'd better get to makeup," Leah said, checking her watch. "See you guys in about an hour?"

"We'll be cheering for you," Jenna told her. "Good luck!"

"Thanks." Leah smiled weakly and rose from her chair, threading her way through the tables and potted palms between the girls' booth and the exit.

Melanie leaned back and pushed her plate away too. She'd eaten more of her breakfast than Leah, but not much. For some reason she'd lost her appetite over the past few days. Nicole had already finished her half grapefruit, and Jenna was wiping up the last of her hollandaise sauce with a forkful of English muffin.

"So what are we doing for the next hour?" Melanie asked. "Any ideas?"

"I want to run over to the rally and see who won the Battle of the Bands," Jenna said. "Whoever did will warm up for Fire & Water tonight." Excitement shone from her face at the mention of the concert, which Leah had promised they'd try to catch part of. "I hope it was your friend, Nicole."

"I said I knew the guy," Nicole corrected irritably. "I didn't say he was a friend."

She was nearly as dressed up that morning as she'd

been the evening before, but in a totally different way, wearing a completely black, completely mod ensemble that simply cried out for sunglasses.

*It must be killing her that we're not eating outside*, Melanie thought, half surprised Nicole hadn't worn dark glasses anyway. She'd always been a fool for trends, but at home she'd never been *this* weird.

"If you're going to the rally, I guess I'll just go upstairs and hang out until the contest," Melanie told Jenna. "There's not enough time for anything else. Are you coming, Nicole?"

Nicole shook her head. "I'm not finished with my tea."

Melanie looked askance at the empty cup.

"I mean, I'm going to have *more* tea," Nicole amended quickly.

"All right. I'll see you guys in the auditorium."

Melanie walked out of the restaurant, thinking what a strange pair Jenna and Nicole made. Of the four girls, those two probably had the most in common, and yet they were so unlike.

*Jenna always seems more in her element with Leah. Or even me. Although the two of us are about as alike as . . .*

Sighing, Melanie refused to finish the thought. She had enough on her mind already without delving into the incredibly depressing differences between her life and Jenna's.

In the lobby, Melanie stopped to look at the things displayed for sale in the hotel gift shop windows. She'd been meaning to check out the store all weekend, but it seemed as though every time she thought of it she was on her way somewhere else. With nothing pressing to do that morning, she looked over the items behind the glass, then walked through the open door.

There were plenty of embroidered T-shirts and the expected coffee mugs, but what Melanie noticed almost immediately was a small framed print on the wall—a watercolor of the Venice boardwalk. She gravitated to it, not in the least put off by its steep price tag. The painting would be the perfect souvenir to remind her of California and her first trip to the beach. But even as she considered buying it as a memento of her time with Brad, Brad wasn't much on her mind.

Jesse was the guy she was thinking of.

*I'll bet he'd like something like this*, she thought, reaching out to run her fingers down the frame. *Something to remind him of home. I ought to buy it for him.*

Or not.

How would she even give it to him? Under what pretense? And what were the chances he'd accept it now that she'd given him back his angel?

Melanie sighed. Buying Jesse a present after everything that had happened between them was probably the dumbest idea she'd ever had. She reached to take the print down from the wall anyway, admiring the painter's style—so different from her own. Something about those cool pastels seemed to shout "California" to her. Would they look the same in Missouri?

*I'm going to find out,* she decided, carrying it to the register. *Jesse and I are still friends, after all. There's no reason I can't give him something.*

But the moment she'd paid for the painting, she hurried to the elevators and rushed upstairs, already filled with doubt.

*Would my heart be racing this way if I wasn't making a big mistake?* she wondered, shutting her hotel room door behind her and leaning against it for support. Removing the print from its paper bag, she looked it over again. *I ought to go right back downstairs and return this.*

But she didn't want to return it.

*I can always keep it for myself if I decide not to give it to Jesse.*

With a quick, guilty flip of the dead bolt, Melanie crossed the room to her still-unmade bed. Flopping her suitcase open on the rumpled blankets, she buried the print between the folded layers of her clothes.

*There,* she thought, zipping the suitcase shut and trying to return her breathing to normal. *For Pete's sake, Andrews, get a grip. It's not that big a deal.*

"Why don't you go on?" Nicole asked Jenna. "You know you want to get to the rally."

But instead of turning around and walking out of the restaurant, as Nicole was praying she would, Jenna hesitated beside their breakfast table. "Are you sure you won't come with me? I mean, how much tea can you drink?"

"I just like it here, all right?"

Nicole was careful not to give herself away by glancing toward the corner. The little round window table was half hidden behind a palm tree, but within seconds of sitting down, Nicole had spotted the head judge and one of her colleagues there despite the fact that the pair had their backs to the room. She'd been watching them ever since, dreaming up ways to approach them. The obvious first step was getting free of her friends, and Jenna was being particularly stubborn.

"Are you sure the waitress knows U.S. Girls is picking up our check?" Jenna asked anxiously, looking around for the woman. "What if she expects you to pay?"

"I'm fine! I can handle it! Will you go to the rally already?" Nicole snapped.

Jenna took a shocked step backward, making Nicole regret her rudeness.

"Look, Jenna, I'm sorry. I just want you to go on without me. Okay?"

*Please!*

Nicole's eyes wandered toward the judges in spite

of her resolutions. At the rate things were moving, they'd leave before Jenna did.

"Fine. I'll see you later," Jenna said coolly.

Nicole felt a twinge as her friend walked away, but she covered it over with quick reassurances. *I need to do this now. I'll make it up to her later.*

She waited until Jenna was out of the room, counted to ten, then got up from the table, her gaze fixed on the pair behind the palm.

*All right, just stay calm. Nice and easy, now.*

Running nervous hands down her black bodysuit and hip-huggers, Nicole smoothed out imaginary wrinkles. The clothes clung to her carefully starved frame, a low-slung silver chain belt emphasizing the flatness of her stomach and the sharpness of her hipbones. High-heeled black boots completed her look, and she moved carefully across the marble-floored restaurant, wary of stepping in anything that might make her slip and look ridiculous.

When Nicole reached their table, the judges were engrossed in a discussion about a bar they'd been to the night before. The head judge's platinum blond head bobbed with laughter as she described some loser she'd met there. With their backs to the room, not only hadn't they observed Nicole's prowl across the restaurant, they didn't even seem to realize she was standing right behind them, hearing every word.

She hesitated, uncertain how to proceed. Should

she walk to the front of their table and interrupt their conversation? The idea made her weak in the knees. But what if they turned around and found her eavesdropping? Wouldn't that be worse?

*This is no time for chickening out*, she thought, taking a deep breath. *It's already Monday morning!*

Clearing her throat loudly, Nicole stepped up beside the nearer judge, an aloof dark-haired woman she hadn't spoken to yet. But when the pair broke off talking to look at her, she very nearly panicked.

"Good morning!" she brayed. "It sure is sunny today!"

The women looked at her as if she were crazy.

"Yes. We can see that," the head judge said, nodding at the window.

Nicole grinned to cover a sickening rush of adrenaline. No one returned her smile.

"This is a nice table," she said. "Nice and private."

"That's the idea, anyway," the dark-haired judge said irritably. "Is there something we can help you with?"

"Um, not really. I just thought I'd say hello."

*Why didn't I think beyond that?* she berated herself. *I should at least have been ready to start a conversation.*

Running her sweaty palms down her body again, Nicole took courage from her hard hipbones.

"Everyone's really excited to see who makes the cut this morning," she said off the top of her head.

The head judge's gaze went from cool to icy. "We're certainly not going to be revealing any finalists before the official announcement."

Nicole's heart nearly stopped as she realized her blunder. They thought she was fishing for clues about the winners!

"No! That wasn't what I—"

"We only have about fifteen minutes before we need to leave for the auditorium," the other woman said, motioning to her half-full plate. "So if you'll be kind enough to excuse us . . ."

"Okay. Sure." Nicole nearly bolted from their table in her haste to abandon the mess she'd made.

*What an idiot you are!* she thought as she hurried through the restaurant. *Why don't you ever think things out in advance?*

She couldn't believe she'd been so stupid as to make the judges think she was asking for secret information!

*And now that I'm running away, they'll be sure that's what I was doing.*

Stopping abruptly, she looked back toward the window table. Her pulse was still racing and her cheeks were on fire, so it was almost a shock to see that the two women had resumed eating as if she'd never been there at all.

*Maybe I didn't blow it so badly after all,* she thought, sidling into the waiting area to watch them. *I've probably blown the entire thing out of proportion. I'll just go back and explain, and everything will be fine.*

Nicole imagined the three of them laughing about the misunderstanding, putting it behind them like old friends. But she didn't move right away. She'd learned her lesson about leaving things to chance the first time. Watching the women from the shelter of a coat tree, she planned a careful strategy.

*I'll just say I was hoping to meet them and I brought up the contest simply for conversation. Honesty is the best policy.*

Her story decided on, Nicole took a couple of deep breaths and set back out the way she'd just come.

*Be confident!* she exhorted herself as she walked up behind the judges. *Be friendly!*

But before she had a chance to be either of those things, she overheard them talking again.

"Have you ever seen anyone more desperate for attention?" the head judge asked. "And that outfit! Is this a restaurant or a costume party?"

"No kidding," the other replied. "That girl's been dogging me all weekend. I've been doing a good job of dodging, but I guess my luck was bound to run out eventually."

*They're talking about me!* Nicole realized, horrified. She froze in place, afraid to even breathe.

The head judge shook her overprocessed head. "Yeah, well, the world is full of wannabes."

"You're not lying!" The other woman chuckled appreciatively. "It's so sad, really. At least this one is skinny."

"Skinny isn't everything. Not by a long shot."

The dark-haired one laughed again. "Poor thing. I'll bet she's really something out in the sticks where she came from."

"If I were her, I'd catch the first flight back, then."

For a moment Nicole didn't think she'd be able to move. Her feet were rooted to the floor, and the whole room reeled as her dreams crashed in, crushing her under their rubble.

Then somehow she managed to spin around. A second later she was fleeing the restaurant, her mortified tears streaming three coats of mascara down her powdered cheeks.

*This is it,* Leah thought, crossing her fingers behind her and resting them on the seat of her jeans.

All the contestants were lined up onstage. At any moment the names of the twenty girls who had made the cut would be revealed.

The head judge walked out to a microphone at center stage, a short list in her hand.

"And the finalists are . . . ," she said, letting the sentence hang so long that Leah half expected the nearest girl to smack her.

" . . . From Wisconsin, Kate Matthews."

"Go, Kate!" a girl screamed from the audience as the beauty Leah had shared her breakfast table with the first day separated herself from the pack and moved to the front of the stage.

144

"From Texas," the judge continued, "Delia Gomez."

Nasty, competitive Delia broke into the most innocent smile imaginable and joined Kate at the edge of the stage.

"From Wyoming, Helen Mayfield."

Leah added a second pair of crossed fingers to the set already behind her back as the judge read down her list, picking up speed as she went. One by one the beaming finalists came forward, while Leah, still at the back of the stage, felt her own smile turning stiff.

What if her name wasn't called?

*If it isn't, then maybe that's for the best,* she thought, breathing deeply as the judge read name after name. *I never wanted to be part of this thing in the first place, so why not end it now?*

"From Missouri, Leah Rosenthal."

"Go, Leah!" Melanie and Jenna screamed from the audience.

For a moment Leah could only smile with relief as a rush of confused emotions ran through her.

*Thank goodness, I made it! . . . Why do I care? . . . Does that mean I want to win now? . . . No, of course not. . . . I just don't want to lose. . . . That's reasonable. . . . Right?*

In a daze she moved forward to take her place with the rest of the finalists, applause and her own heartbeat pounding in her ears.

# Twelve

"Please give *all* of our contestants a warm round of applause," the head judge said, directing hers toward the losers at the back of the stage.

Nicole had already clapped for Leah. Now she just wanted to get out of the auditorium before she had to talk to anyone—especially one of the judges. She lurched up out of her seat and began stumbling blindly over the knees between her and the aisle.

"Hey, where are you going?" Melanie called after her. "Are you going to meet me at the pool?"

During breakfast that morning the two of them had discussed fitting in some last-minute tanning if Leah had to attend the finalists' meeting. At the time it had seemed like a good idea, but now being anywhere in public was the last thing Nicole wanted. She didn't answer Melanie—didn't even turn her head—as she beat a path to the exit.

For the past hour and a half, ever since she'd overheard the judges talking about her, she'd barely managed to pretend to be fine. She'd run straight from the restaurant to her room, hurriedly locking the adjoining door in case Melanie or Jenna showed up. With Leah downstairs getting ready to compete, Nicole had cried her eyes red before she'd scrubbed off what was left of her makeup. The black clothes she had chosen so carefully that morning she'd ripped off and tossed on the floor, replacing them with a plain blue silk shirt and rumpled jeans. Lastly, she'd forced a brush through her hair-sprayed curls until they were loose and nearly straight again.

*I don't care what I look like anymore*, she'd thought, blinking at her bare face and flyaway hair through more tears. *What difference does it make?*

The realization that it no longer made any difference at all had started her sobbing anew. *It's over*, she'd told herself despairingly, barely able to believe how it had ended. *All her hopes, so many dreams . . .*

Half a bottle of Visine later, she'd shoved her bare feet into sneakers, filled a pants pocket with tissues, and gone down to the auditorium, where she'd arrived late enough to avoid talking much. Now, slipping back out through its doors, she could feel the tears welling up again. All she wanted was a quiet place to hide until her plane took off the next morning.

*Except that now I'll have to go to Leah's contest tonight. And probably Jenna's stupid concert if the contest ends early enough. Not to mention the big bus tour this afternoon . . .*

Beating the crowd into the hall, Nicole hurried through the lobby on her way to the elevators. If she could just get upstairs before Melanie did, she could make sure the adjoining door was still locked, then keep so quiet that no one would even know she was—

"Nicole? Nicole, is that you?"

She stopped at the sound of her name and turned reluctantly toward the voice.

"It's you! I can't believe it!" Guy Vaughn exclaimed, rushing over to meet her. "I didn't know you were here!"

Nicole tried to smile. "Hi, Guy."

"When I saw you walking across the lobby, I thought I was seeing things," he said excitedly, looking her up and down. "I mean, we're a long way from Clearwater Crossing, and you look so—"

"Awful," she said quickly, not wanting to hear it from him. "I know."

"Awful? No way! I was going to say different. Your clothes, your hair. It's all just a lot . . . less. I like it."

"You *like* it?" she repeated, dumbfounded. "This is the worst I've looked all weekend!"

He shrugged. "What do I know? I only know what I like."

"I heard you sing last night," she said, eager to change the subject. "Your band is really good."

Guy glanced away, embarrassed. "Well, you know what they say: It's better to be lucky than good. I still can't believe we won."

"Luck had nothing to do with it," she said, surprised to hear herself insisting.

"All the same," he said with a smile, "I can't believe we're opening for Fire & Water tonight."

"Yeah. Congratulations."

They stood staring at each other, temporarily out of things to say. It seemed Guy had gotten taller since she'd seen him last, which was impossible, since it hadn't even been a month. He looked different, though. Cuter, maybe. More confident . . .

*You're imagining things*, she told herself. *You're the one who's different.* She could barely believe she was the same person who had boarded that plane to Los Angeles not even three days before.

"Wow," Guy said at last. "It's fantastic to see you here. I wouldn't have expected you to come to a rally like this."

"What?" Nicole said, startled. "Oh, no. A friend of mine's competing in the U.S. Girls thing, and she brought three of us as her guests."

"The modeling contest." There was a subtle but definite change in his expression. His eyes went blank; his mouth went firm. All of a sudden he looked *exactly* the way she'd remembered him. "Of course! You're really here for the modeling contest."

Nicole winced, sure what was on his mind. *Great*, she thought, more tears about to start. *Now I'm shallow again.*

"I—I've got to go," she stammered, not about to let Guy see her cry. "I've . . . Bye."

Wheeling around before he could reply, she ran straight past the elevators and down the hall to the rest room, where she locked herself into the first empty stall. All she wanted was to be alone and cry herself hoarse in private.

Pulling her feet up so no one could see them, she buried her face in her arms until both of her wishes came true.


"Aaaahhh!" Melanie shouted, bolting upright on her lounge chair by the swimming pool. "What the . . . Brad!"

Grabbing one corner of her towel, she wiped the ice water off her belly while Brad laughed at his prank.

"Only a tourist would sunbathe out here in January," he teased. "I couldn't resist."

He was dressed for work in his white coat and black pants. Melanie was half tempted to push him backward into the pool and see how funny he thought *that* was.

"That water was cold," she said sulkily instead, pulling a shirt on over her bikini. "I already had goose bumps."

"I wish I had time to warm you up."

The hungry way his eyes roamed her body did a better job than he probably could have imagined, but she lifted her chin a little, determined not to show it. "You mean you wish you had the chance. Guys always find the time."

"I'll bet they do," he agreed with an impish grin. "Which reminds me, what are we doing tonight?"

"Leah made the contest cut, so I'm going to the finals."

"Oh," he said, downcast. "I mean, I'm glad for your friend. But I was really hoping . . ."

"I know. Me too."

The night before had been something to remember. She and Brad had danced at the rally awhile, but when Melanie had made an offhand remark about ice cream, he'd hustled her off to a hotel kitchen and bummed two sundaes from his boss. They'd eaten them in a storage room, where Brad had entertained her with a drum solo on the pots and pans.

Afterward, they'd taken his car into the Hollywood Hills. From the relative darkness of winding Mulholland Drive, the lights of the city had spread out beneath them like scattered handfuls of colored glass. Melanie had been so enthralled with the view that Brad had dipped down, crossed the freeway, and taken her up again on the other side.

"This is the Griffith Park Observatory," he'd said pulling into a parking lot and hustling her out of the car. "Ever see *Rebel Without a Cause?*"

Melanie had nodded, catching her breath at the sight of the famous white building with the big black dome. They'd walked its walled observation deck above the city, talking of James Dean and tragic love and how stupid it was to race cars on the street, until at last the words had run out and Brad had taken her into his arms. Melanie knew she'd never forget how safe she'd felt there, or the way he'd taken his time with his kisses. Her skin broke into goose bumps again at the mere recollection.

Brad sat down on the edge of her lounge chair and put an arm around her, pulling her close to his side. "What a drag," he said. "I was hoping we'd have one more night."

"I know," she repeated. "Me too. I can't believe we're leaving tomorrow. It seems like we just got here."

"Speaking of 'we,'" Brad said, glancing at the empty chairs around her, "where are all your friends?"

"Leah had to go to a finalists' meeting and Jenna's at the rally. I don't know where Nicole is—she was supposed to meet me here."

"Maybe she came to her senses," Brad teased. "It's not that warm today."

Melanie sighed. "The sun is pretty warm, but it's like there's nothing behind it, you know? Every time a cloud blows across or something it's freezing."

The temperature had dropped at least ten degrees since Saturday, and the crowd at the pool was down to a couple of diehards. "I've just gotten so pale this year. I was hoping to pick up some color."

Brad gave her another squeeze. "Listen very carefully to what I'm about to tell you," he said, locking his gaze with hers. "Tanning booths. They have them in the hotel gym."

"Is that how you stay so dark?"

"Don't," he replied with a mischievous smile. "You'll take all the mystery out of our relationship."

A hundred snide comebacks sprang to mind at his use of the word 'relationship', but for some reason she didn't feel like using any of them.

"I'll miss you tonight," she said instead, realizing as the words spilled out just how true they were. "I guess, well . . . Is this the last time I'll see you?"

"Not if you don't want it to be." His face was very near hers. His eyes were serious. "I know I don't."

"But you have to work, and by the time you get off I'll be going to the contest. Then tomorrow our plane leaves first thing."

"I'll find you," Brad promised. "Sometime between now and then . . . There's no way I'm letting you go without saying good-bye."

Melanie nuzzled into his side and hugged him. Brad was so warm, so solid. It didn't seem fair that she'd only just found him and now she had to let him go.

If only he lived in Missouri! She could imagine them taking long walks together through the snowy woods, or snuggling in front of a roaring fire. In the summer they'd go to the lake, to her brook, to the drive-in. . . .

She could almost see herself falling in love.

*I ought to give him that picture I bought for Jesse.* The thought popped into her head out of nowhere. *The print would mean more to Brad than to Jesse, and it would be something to remember me by.*

After all, Brad was the one who had taken her to Venice. The symbolism of the print would be obvious to him.

"I have something for you," she blurted out impulsively.

"I have something for you, too."

"Really? What?"

"This," Brad said, lowering his lips to hers.

He kissed her gently but insistently, melting her resistance until she kissed him back. Her arms tightened around him, her teeth tugged at his lower lip. . . .

"Whew!" he said, pulling away. "Too much of that and I'll have to take another shower before I clock in."

Melanie smiled, not loosening her grip.

"So what did you have for me?" he asked.

"Huh?" she said, startled. "Oh. Right."

But what had seemed like a good plan a moment before now seemed like a horribly bad one.

*I can't give him a present from the place where he works. He's probably seen that picture a thousand times. If he wanted it, he'd have bought it by now.*

Except that it *was* pretty pricey.

*All the more reason. If he knows what I paid, he might*

154

*be embarrassed to take it.* The last thing she wanted was to end their time together with an awkward scene.

*It just doesn't make sense to give him Jesse's picture.*

Melanie sighed. Nothing made sense anymore.

"So?" Brad prompted. "I'm waiting."

"You're not going to believe this," Melanie said slowly, making it up as she went along. "But I have the same thing for you that you had for me."

A pleased grin broke out on his face. "Perfect," he said, leaning down to kiss her again.

But Melanie braced her hands against his chest, keeping him away.

"No, the next time I see you," she told him. "That way I know I'll see you again."

He cupped her cheek with one large hand, his eyes looking deep into hers. "Oh, you'll see me again," he promised.

# *Thirteen*

W*ell, this is it,* Leah thought, leaving her last contestants' meeting. *One more event and it's over.*

Win or lose, there was no denying that having the U.S. Girls contest behind her would be an incredible relief.

Except that if she won, it would really just be the beginning. For the past hour the twenty finalists had been learning about the various commitments they'd be expected to fulfill if they became one of the five winning U.S. Girls. Between the modeling and the appearances, Leah wondered when the judges thought the winners would use their college scholarships. Not that she expected they'd lost much sleep over that question.

She wandered through the lobby in a daze on her way to meet her friends in their hotel rooms. They were going to have some lunch. Then, in the afternoon, U.S. Girls was taking everyone on a two-hour sightseeing tour.

Leah's steps slowed as she passed through the reception area. It seemed impossible that it was already the third morning since she'd checked in at that very counter, and tomorrow morning she'd be checking out again.

*At least I made the cut*, she thought. *Whatever happens from here on out, I can hold up my head when I get home.*

A clerk bustled around behind the massive desk while a young couple waited in front, surrounded by piles of luggage.

"Are you happy?" Leah heard the man ask.

"Of course," his companion replied with a Southern drawl. Hanging from one of his arms, she gazed adoringly into his eyes. "Are you?"

"I'd be an idiot if I wasn't." He pulled her into an embrace and kissed her just as the clerk turned to face them.

"Here you are, Mr. and Mrs. Jackson," he said, passing some items over the counter. "All set, and I've called a bellboy to help you with your luggage."

The pair broke apart, smiling.

"Mrs. Jackson!" the woman giggled to her husband.

"We're so glad you've chosen to spend your honeymoon here," the clerk went on. "If there's anything you need to make your stay more comfortable, please don't hesitate to ask."

Mr. Jackson reached forward to take their room key. "Thanks, but I've got everything I need right here."

"David!" His new wife laughed and slapped his arm playfully, the diamond on her left hand glittering.

Leah had abandoned any pretense of walking. Instead she lurked by a palm tree near the opposite wall, watching.

"Where are you kids from?" an elderly woman in line behind the couple asked.

"Louisiana, can you believe it?" the new Mrs. Jackson replied, turning to face the woman. Her smile was radiant as she gestured to the luggage at her feet. "We're going to be here two weeks!"

"Well, now, that's real nice," the lady said. "You kids make an awfully cute couple."

David reached for his wife possessively. "Cutest girl in Baton Rouge," he bragged. "I'm a lucky guy."

Leah felt like a voyeur, standing there spying on someone else's life, but wasn't the nice woman giving the newlyweds the third degree just as bad? And it wasn't as if no one else was checking them out, either; the happy couple was the center of attention for the entire lobby. Everyone who passed by at least glanced their way, many stopping to stare openly. They were just so young, and cute, and sloppily in love.

Leah's hand crept to the ring around her neck. *That could be me*, she realized, squeezing the silver hard. *I could be that girl. Me and Miguel, checking into a hotel, starting our new life together . . .*

The idea was overwhelming in its simplicity. All this time she'd been trying to make the future so hard, and it just wasn't.

*We wouldn't come here, though. We'd go to Venice, or Paris, or somewhere else where we don't even speak the language. And we'd get some incredibly romantic room with a view. . . .*

The thought of a private room with Miguel did strange things to her pulse. *And we'd be married, so no one could look down on us, or check up on us, or tell us what to do. Anything we wanted . . .*

Her hand squeezed the ring until it bruised her palm, and finally she understood what it was. Not jewelry—she'd known that—but also not the pledge of love she'd taken it for. The ring was a ticket, a ticket to adulthood and all it held. Freedom, self-reliance, love . . .

Fumbling with its ribbon, Leah flipped the ring to the outside of her shirt and slipped it onto her left ring finger. Over the course of the weekend she'd had it on most of her other fingers, but until that very moment she'd refused to try the only one that mattered. Now she stared down at the gleaming circle of silver, mesmerized, afraid of how right it looked there.

Was she crazy not to at least *consider* marrying Miguel?

\* \* \*

"Look, Nicole!" Jenna squealed, pointing at the sidewalk beneath her feet. "Look whose star it is!"

Nicole didn't have enough energy left even to pretend she was interested. Being depressed was tiring enough, but trying to hide it was exhausting. And that was before they'd walked probably a mile down Hollywood Boulevard from the stacked discs of the Capitol Records building, where their tour bus had parked, looking at all the stars immortalized in pink and gray paving.

"Just tell me," Nicole replied, not moving. "I'm not taking another step."

Melanie snorted. "Then good luck getting back to the bus. I doubt they're coming down here to pick you up."

"Whose is it, Jenna?" Leah asked, walking over to see for herself.

She and Melanie both looked where Jenna pointed and immediately started laughing.

"No excuses, Nicole. You *have* to see this," said Leah. "Better still, we have to get someone to take our picture."

Melanie was already fishing her camera out of her bag. "Come on, Nicole. Don't be a spoilsport."

Sighing deeply, Nicole dragged herself to the spot on the sidewalk where the other three girls had gathered. TOM CRUISE, said the brass-edged pink star. Nicole didn't even smile.

"It's him! It's really him!" Jenna cried goofily, grabbing her by one arm and jumping up and down as though she'd just spotted the genuine article.

"Wow. And we didn't even have to chase him!" Leah added.

Melanie stopped a middle-aged couple loaded down with shopping bags. "Excuse me. Would you mind taking our picture?"

The woman set her bags on the pavement. "You girls just tell me when you're ready."

Melanie handed her the camera and showed her which button to press while Leah posed everyone.

"Nicole, you and Melanie kneel right behind the star, and get your faces low to the ground. Jenna and I'll crouch behind you."

The next thing Nicole knew, her chin was being pressed down onto the white-flecked gray concrete and Leah's elbow was bruising her back.

"Look! I'm posing with Tom and Nicole!" Leah quipped.

"Say cheese!" the lady with the camera instructed, snapping the picture.

"Great. Thanks a lot!" Melanie scrambled up to retrieve her camera.

The older couple waved and went on their way.

"We'd better get back to the bus," Leah said, checking her watch. "It's getting pretty late."

The girls started up the sidewalk on the long trek to their ride, but Nicole lagged behind, wanting to be by herself. After only a minute, however, Jenna dropped back beside her.

"Is everything okay?" she asked, her blue eyes worried.

"Of course," Nicole lied quickly. "Why wouldn't it be?"

"I don't know. You don't seem happy. And this morning, in the restaurant—"

"I already said I was sorry about this morning. There was just something I wanted to do."

"And did you do it?"

For a moment the story of her humiliation filled her mouth, ready to tumble out. Jenna would be sure to sympathize. But then Nicole glanced ahead and changed her mind. She might humble herself to Jenna, or even to Leah, but never to Melanie.

"Yes, and it was nothing, all right?"

"If you say so."

The two of them walked in silence, the showy sights of the boulevard completely lost on Nicole.

*This should have been my big moment*, she thought, her sneakers dragging over the stars. *I should be on top of the world right now.*

Instead she was as low as she'd ever been, just going through the motions until she could run home with her tail between her legs.

"You'll like the movie stars' homes better," Jenna said consolingly as they reached the group climbing back onto their bus. "You won't have to walk at all."

"Sure."

Nicole blinked hard as she wound her way through the crush of contestants and guests on the bus, looking for her seat near the back. She'd thought she was all out of tears, but if Jenna persisted in being so nice . . .

Nicole dropped into her seat, glad of the din around her. Leah's group had been assigned to a bus filled mostly with finalists and their friends, and everyone was in high spirits, looking forward to the evening's competition. All over the vehicle girls were kneeling in their seats, laughing and shouting to each other about the things they'd seen and done so far on the tour. Mercifully, no one could expect Nicole to carry on a conversation under such conditions; she only had to keep up the act a little longer before they went back to the hotel.

The first hour of the tour had included a drive around the main sights of the city, including the Hollywood Bowl, a street with good views of the Hollywood sign, and the outside of the house seen in *Happy Days*. From there the bus had dropped them at the top of the Walk of Fame, where they'd walked to the Hollywood Wax Museum and Ripley's Believe It or Not! They'd ended at Mann's Chinese Theater, touring the inside and checking out the footprints in the concrete before wandering the last couple of blocks down the walk in search of their favorite "stars." Now everyone crowded back into their seats for the last event on the itinerary—a drive-by tour of celebrities' homes in Beverly Hills.

"I hope we see someone famous out in their yard," Melanie said, dropping into the seat beside Leah and twisting around to talk to Nicole and Jenna in the row behind her.

"That *would* be cool," said Jenna. "But if buses were driving by your house all day, would you ever come outside?"

"Heck no," said Melanie. "I'd probably move."

Leah made a face. "For all we know, they're just going to drive us by a bunch of random houses and *pretend* that movie stars live there. Who's going to call them liars?"

The bus engine sprang to life, adding to the noise inside and setting the vehicle vibrating. The girls not already seated scrambled for their places, while the others ignored the disturbance and continued their conversations.

From her seat near the back, Nicole had a clear view of the gorgeous faces all over the bus. What an idiot she was to have thought she could be a model! Looking around her now, she felt the full weight of her delusion. Every single contestant there was better-looking than she was—most of their *friends* were better-looking—and of the fifty girls who had started out, ninety percent would be losers.

If they hadn't lost already.

Her eyes newly opened, Nicole couldn't believe

she'd once thought herself as attractive as the crowd all around her.

*I wish I could just crawl into a hole somewhere and die*, she thought as the bus began to move.

Girls who had been kneeling in their seats hurried to sit down. Melanie and Leah turned to face the front. And then Jenna's arm slipped across her shoulders.

"Feel better," she whispered, giving Nicole's arms a squeeze. "I can't stand to see you so down."

Nicole tried to shake her off, but Jenna's sympathy was insistent.

"Don't," Nicole said desperately. "I'm fine."

"You don't look fine."

Nicole turned to argue, a lie on her lips, but there was no looking into Jenna's eyes and repeating that nothing was wrong. Her friend had clearly picked up on her mood, if not the reason for it. Tears filled Nicole's eyes again, making Jenna look blurry.

"If you're really my friend," Nicole whispered, "you'll drop this before you make me cry."

Jenna removed her arm. "All right," she said with obvious reluctance. "But I'm right here if you need me. Don't forget."

"I won't," Nicole sniffed, feeling a tear roll down her cheek. She hurriedly wiped it away, squeezing her eyes shut against the flood that ached to follow.

And when Jenna's arm crept back again, she didn't even object.

# *Fourteen*

"Leah Rosenthal, Missouri," the announcer called, prompting the mandatory applause from the crowd in the auditorium.

Leah barely heard the noise as she came out onto the stage to show off her green evening dress, dry-cleaned courtesy of the hotel. She had already modeled her jeans, but in the finals the girls were expected to change clothes and model twice. Now she crossed the stage for the second time, her heart hammering in her chest.

"Go, Leah!" Jenna cried from the crowd, ignoring the air of formality that had descended for the finals. With the contest down to its last event, the tension in the room was palpable.

Leah tried to smile in the direction of her friends, but her lips seemed stuck on her teeth, quivering halfway up. She couldn't believe how nervous she was! Her legs felt like jelly as she reached the front of the stage to pose for the judges, and for the first time she understood why the other girls were always worried about slipping and falling. Walking was definitely harder when a person couldn't feel her feet. Eyes dazzled by the beam of the spotlight, Leah let her gaze skim blindly over the audience as she made her by now practiced turns.

*What are you getting so worked up about? Just stay calm,* she thought as she posed. But her hands were so sweaty she was afraid Miguel's ring might slip off her thumb and go clattering across the stage. She closed the fingers of her left hand around it, knowing she couldn't look graceful with a fist clenched at her side, not knowing what else to do.

And then the announcer called the next girl's name and Leah found herself walking to her mark at the back of the stage. She'd come out early in the lineup for jeans, so she was nearly last for the evening dresses. There were only two girls left. Another name was called.

Only one left.

The last girl walked onstage. Leah felt the line of finalists stiffen as they realized how close to the end they were. By the time the girl finished posing and walked over to join them, Leah felt light-headed. She remembered the stories she'd heard about people blacking out at weddings from standing so long under stress.

*Just breathe and you'll be all right.* But the moment she had the thought, it seemed her body actually

167

forgot how to take in air on its own. She had to help with every breath, her knees shaking more all the time.

Then the spotlight, which had been picking out girls one by one, began sweeping dizzily back and forth across the entire line of twenty. The crowd burst into excited applause, which grew as the head judge approached the podium to stand beside the tuxedoed announcer, an envelope in her hand.

"Once again, I'd like to thank you all for joining us for this very special occasion," she began slowly, giving every indication that she planned to take her time.

Leah could barely suppress the groan that rose inside her chest. *No more pointless remarks!* she thought desperately.

Glancing sideways down the line, she saw that most of the other girls' nerves seemed stretched as tightly as hers.

"As you know, this is the first time our company has tried this, and we wanted to be absolutely sure the contest would result not just in five winners, but in five *true* U.S. Girls—girls we are proud to have represent us."

The contestant on Leah's left actually whimpered a little.

"It is my pleasure to say," the judge continued, "that we feel we've accomplished that goal. And in fact, there are more than five girls on this stage tonight whom we'd be happy to use in our campaign."

She stopped long enough to smile at the contestants before she returned her attention to the audience and held up her stark white envelope. "We've narrowed it down to five anyway."

The audience chuckled tensely. Leah sucked in her breath as the judge ran a thumbnail beneath the red seal on the envelope. Slowly, smiling the whole time, the woman drew out a plain white card.

"Are you ready?" she asked the audience.

People applauded to show that they were, and Leah gave up trying to breathe. Surely she could go without oxygen for the length of time it took to read five names.

"Very well. And before I reveal any names, let me be the first to congratulate the winners."

The judge turned her back on the audience again. "Are *you* ready?" she asked the finalists.

*Could she drag this out any longer?*

Leah was imagining ways to get back at the woman when the name of the first winner finally tumbled through the speakers.

"From Oklahoma, Ms. Eileen Capshaw!"

A scream split the ranks of the finalists. Leah looked down the row to see Eileen's hands covering her face as her whole body shook with emotion. The crowd applauded wildly. The contestants on either side congratulated her, hoping to more truly share her joy in a moment. Eventually she pulled herself together enough to walk out and be hugged by the judge, streaming tears in spite of her smile.

"Congratulations!" the judge cooed as the announcer handed Eileen a bouquet of roses.

Waving to the cheering crowd, still shaking, Eileen walked to center stage to await the rest of the winners.

The judge bent toward the microphone again. "From Utah, Ms. Megan Lowe!"

More screams, more applause. Leah felt her toes cramp up inside her shoes.

"From Texas," the judge continued, "Ms. Delia Gomez!"

*Delia made it?*

Leah watched, stunned, as the Texas beauty strutted out to collect her prize. No hysterics for Delia—no screams, no smiles. The smirk on her face seemed to say she'd been expecting to win all along. Leah hadn't expected it, though. As far as she was concerned, any girl onstage would have been a better choice. Delia's looks were all right, but as far as inner beauty went . . .

"From New York, Ms. Bethany Chee!"

A pronounced change of attitude affected the remaining finalists as Bethany joined the winners. Gone were the polite applause, the confident smiles. Everyone knew that only one more name would follow. All sixteen girls stood up straighter, steeling themselves against a disappointment that was almost sure to follow. Leah drew a deep breath.

"And our final U.S. Girl . . . ," the judge announced, pausing dramatically. "From Wisconsin! Ms. Kate Matthews!"

Leah was aware of her own palms slapping together. She heard the crowd roar as the five winners took a bow. But for a moment she didn't feel anything. She was numb, her smile frozen on her face.

The contest was over. She hadn't won. There would be no scholarship from U.S. Girls.

On Leah's right, the contestant from California was crying openly. The one on her left looked shell-shocked.

*So this is what it comes down to,* Leah thought. *After all this time, after everything I've been through, it's over just like that.*

She was no longer a U.S. Girl.

And suddenly the feeling charged back into her body. She had sensation in her hands again as she brought them together with total enthusiasm. She didn't need to remind herself to breathe anymore—breath filled her entire body. She'd never felt more alive. Abandoning her clapping, she brought her fingers up to her mouth and blew, sounding the ear-splitting whistle she'd learned from Jenna. A few of the other losing contestants turned shocked expressions her way, but what did she care? She was done. She was free!

And when Jenna's answering whistle came back from the audience, it was all Leah could do not to bolt off the stage to share her relief with her friends. She never had to model again! An enormous weight had been lifted from her shoulders. And as far as the scholarship went, well . . .

Leah glanced down at Miguel's ring and smiled. *Maybe I don't need to be in such a hurry to go to college after all.*

As inconspicuously as she could, she started edging toward the wings, eager to get off the stage and on with the rest of her life.

If they hurried, they could still catch most of Jenna's concert.

"Isn't this great?" Jenna shouted to Leah.

"Yeah. I'm really glad we could make it."

All four girls were standing in front of their seats at the Fire & Water concert, but their row was so close to the back that no one behind them complained. Those people were on their feet too, half of them dancing in place to the music that pulsed through the theater. They had missed Trinity's warm-up set, but Fire & Water was only four or five songs into its performance, and the crowd was at peak energy, singing, stomping, and whistling for favorites. Colored stage lights illuminated the five members of the band, while strobes flashed out into the audience.

"I knew you'd like them!" Jenna shouted happily. "I can't believe we're here!"

When Leah's name hadn't been called with the winners, Jenna hadn't known how to react. At first she hadn't believed it—how could they not have picked Leah? And Leah had looked so stunned that Jenna's heart had almost broken for her. Then a familiar smile had appeared on Leah's face, her fingers had gone to her lips, and with one piercing whistle she'd told the world she was fine. It couldn't have been a minute later that she'd begun surreptitiously pointing to an exit door, signaling her friends to meet her outside.

And now here they were at the concert: Leah still in her contest dress, Nicole setting her weekend record for the longest time in any single outfit with the jeans and blue blouse she'd changed into that morning. Melanie had on a black dress; Jenna, good slacks and a blazer.

*Between us we've got fashion covered*, Jenna thought with a smile.

Although she had to admit it bothered her to see Nicole so dressed down. Not that there was anything wrong with it. Half the people in the theater were wearing denim. But it didn't seem normal for Nicole— especially not after the razzing she'd given Jenna for wearing jeans earlier in the weekend.

"What do you think?" Jenna shouted to her over the music. "Pretty good, aren't they?"

Nicole nodded dully.

"I wish we could have seen your friend play. Uh, I mean that guy you know," Jenna amended quickly.

But unlike earlier that morning, Nicole barely even reacted. "Yeah. Oh well."

Jenna tried one more time. "There's Kei," she said, pointing to the drummer. "I still can't believe I met her."

"Uh-huh."

Nicole was clearly lost somewhere, buried in herself, and after a moment Jenna let her go.

*I can't force her to tell me what's wrong if she doesn't want to.*

Instead she gave Nicole an encouraging smile, waved to Melanie on Nicole's other side, and turned her attention back to the stage just as Fire & Water segued into another song, its current radio hit.

"Oh, I *love* this song!" Jenna cried. Her voice was lost in the roar from the crowd as they recognized it too.

Jenna swayed on her feet, giving herself to the music. The song was a ballad, and while a casual listener might have mistaken the words for a standard love song, Jenna knew the love being sung about was anything but standard. She mouthed the lyrics as if she had written them herself, not caring that she and her friends had lousy seats, or that the band looked like ants down onstage. She was there, she could hear, and she felt incredibly grateful.

As the song came to a close, Kei spoke its title as if it were a command. "Make a wish," she breathed.

And Jenna closed her eyes and did.

# *Fifteen*

*F*ire & Water was just beginning its encore when Nicole felt a tap on her shoulder. "Do you girls want to dance?"

She turned her head irritably, ready to brush off whatever fool had dared. Except that the fool was Guy. And when she saw him standing there, she didn't know what to do.

"I, uh . . . Where?" she stammered stupidly.

Guy and his two bandmates had managed to work their way down the row of seats behind Nicole's. Now he pointed toward a large level area behind the last row. "Come on. The concert's almost over. No one will care."

Nicole stayed where she was, desperate for an excuse. "I can't. There are four of us and only three of you. I can't leave one of my friends."

"I'll dance with her!" offered a total stranger Guy had squeezed in on.

"There you go!" Guy told her. "Problem solved."

"Well, I'll have to ask them if they *want* to dance . . ." Nicole stalled, grasping at the last straw.

The night before, after she'd seen Guy sing, she'd have jumped at such an unexpected opportunity to make a better impression on him. But a lot had changed since then, and the last thing she needed now was a dose of Guy's sanctimonious attitude.

"Of course I want to dance!" Jenna put in excitedly, not waiting for Nicole to ask her. She turned to Melanie and Leah. "Okay, you guys?"

"Why not?" Melanie replied.

Leah was already starting down the row to the spot Guy had pointed out.

Nicole followed her friends reluctantly while Guy and his group struggled down the row behind.

"I love this song!" Jenna said, beginning to dance before partners were even discussed.

One of Guy's friends paired up with her, Leah grabbed the other one, and Melanie danced with the volunteer. Not knowing what else to do, Nicole began to dance as well, leaving Guy to follow along.

To her amazement, he was a fantastic dancer. Nicole had always thought her own dancing was pretty good, but Guy was so natural, so in charge of every move, that soon she felt self-conscious about how poorly she must compare.

*What next?* she thought bitterly. *Now I can't even dance right.*

She tried a little harder all the same, but by the end of the second song she was so busy watching Guy she'd practically forgotten that anyone might be watching her.

"We're going to do one more song for you tonight," a member of Fire & Water announced. Nicole thought the voice was probably the lead singer's, but she could barely see the stage anymore for all the people who had crowded onto their makeshift dance floor.

"This is one of my favorites," the voice continued, "and I hope one of yours too."

The crowd roared in affirmation as the band began to play.

"Oh, I love this!" Jenna shouted. "They had to play this one!"

Except that it was a slow song. The small measure of relaxation Nicole had finally achieved disappeared at the very first chord.

*Now what?* she worried. All around her, people were pairing up to dance—and she didn't want to slow-dance with Guy.

But when he stretched out his hands to her, she stepped forward anyway, only to face another surprise: Guy's arms weren't such a horrible place to be.

He held her securely but not too close. His arms were strong but not constricting. Nicole had the sense that if she were to stumble, he'd catch her, but that he'd let go just as quickly if she wanted to get free. Their faces were so close together, she suddenly realized that she'd never really looked at him before. Not straight into his eyes, anyway. And the way he was looking at her was almost breathtaking, as though he were seeing her for the first time too.

When the song came to an end, Nicole was almost sorry to let go, but Guy dropped his arms immediately to applaud for the band. Jenna and Leah joined in with more of those ear-splitting whistles, and Melanie gave it a try as well, although she hadn't mastered it yet. Nicole clapped absently, her gaze still on Guy. She was sorry now that she'd missed hearing his band perform earlier that night. It would have been something to see him on that big stage, singing in front of so many people.

Fire & Water took its final bows and walked off. This time the house lights came up immediately, signaling that there wouldn't be a second encore. The entire audience was on its feet, still applauding, but eventually the noise died down and people began to wander toward the exits.

"Can I walk you back to the hotel?" Guy asked.

Nicole glanced toward her friends. Jenna was still whistling her heart out, and Melanie and Leah were attempting to talk to the guys they had danced with. *They'll be fine without me*, she decided. *I'll see them back at the hotel*.

Outside, the air was cold enough to make Nicole desperately wish she had brought a jacket. She hugged her chest and ran her hands up and down her arms as she and Guy walked the long block to the hotel.

"You should have brought a coat," Guy said, but

he didn't offer to put his arm around her, the way a lot of other guys would have.

*Of course not. He's not interested in you*, she thought, feeling stupid for even considering it.

At last they reached a side entrance to the hotel. Nicole pushed gratefully through it into the heated air, not waiting to see if Guy would open the door for her.

"Brrr!" she exclaimed, trying to shake off the cold.

Guy shrugged. "You have to admit, it's still pretty nice out compared to the weather back home."

Nicole didn't answer as they walked down the hall toward the lobby. As eager as she was to leave L.A., the thought of home wasn't too appealing. Everyone she knew would be waiting to ask her about the contest, expecting a blow-by-blow account, because— like a total idiot—she'd *told* everyone about her trip before she'd left for California. How she wished now she had bragged a little less!

*Better yet, I wish I'd never come. Courtney wouldn't be mad at me, for one thing. I wouldn't be grounded when I get back. And I'd have never met those awful judges. . . .*

"Do you want to get some hot chocolate or something?" she asked Guy as they entered the lobby. "I'd love to sit by that fire."

She nodded toward the far corner of the room, where a glowing stone fireplace was surrounded by red velvet chairs.

"You're drinking hot chocolate now? Last time I hung out with you it was diet soda."

She'd actually meant that *he* should have hot chocolate, but looking into his amused blue eyes, she knew she had to call his bluff.

"Hot chocolate," she said firmly. "And one of those big cinnamon rolls."

*After all, what difference does it make?* she thought miserably as they paid for their purchases at the snack cart in the lobby. Moving to the counter at the side of the cart, she poured coffee creamer into her cocoa, making it even richer.

"I've never seen anyone do that before," Guy said, picking up the creamer to give it a try. "It looks good, though."

"It is," she said almost grimly. She hadn't done it herself in more than a year.

Balancing her cinnamon roll on top, Nicole picked up her cup in one hand and grabbed some napkins and a plastic fork with the other. She glanced at Guy to make sure he was following, then set off across the marble floor to the chair nearest the fire.

"I wonder why no one else is here," she said, setting her hot chocolate down on an end table and tearing into her sweet roll.

Guy glanced at his watch. "It's late."

"I guess everyone's packing to go home tomorrow."

"I'm looking forward to getting home myself— not that this hasn't been an incredible experience."

"It's been incredible, all right," she said sarcastically. Too late, she wished she'd kept that remark to herself.

"What do you mean?" Guy asked. The firelight played on his face as he leaned forward, making their corner of the lobby seem cozier and more private than it really was. "You didn't have a good time this weekend?"

Nicole hesitated, tempted to lie. How could she tell Guy what had happened to her?

On the other hand, how could she tell anyone else? She couldn't bear to look so foolish in front of her friends in Eight Prime, and if she ever breathed a word to Courtney she'd never live it down. At least Guy didn't go to her school.

"No," she admitted. "I had a lousy time this weekend."

"You didn't like the modeling contest?"

"It's not that. I mean, it is . . . but it's so much more complicated than that. I couldn't even tell you. You'd think I was crazy."

"Or I might understand completely. You never know."

She shook her head before she realized that if anyone ought to understand, it was Guy. With little left to lose, she decided to take a shot.

"Did you ever think that maybe . . . well, like, maybe God was sending you a sign about something?" she asked in a rush.

She wouldn't have been surprised if he had laughed, or dismissed the question completely. If he'd shown the least sign of ridicule, she was ready to drop the whole thing. But the interest in his eyes only deepened. He leaned a bit farther forward, putting his elbows on his knees.

"Yes," he said levelly. "Absolutely."

She took a deep breath for courage. "Well, I actually thought God wanted me to come here this weekend."

"Go on," he urged.

"You know how everyone was giving me a hard time about my dieting? But models *have* to be thin. So I asked God to send me a sign—to say if I was doing the right thing or not—and the next thing I know, I'm invited to California for this entire modeling weekend. Not only that, but my parents give me a brand-new suitcase for no apparent reason. It was textbook. I was absolutely certain God wanted me to come to L.A. so he could fix me up with a modeling assignment. Pretty stupid, huh?"

"I, uh, take it that isn't what happened," Guy said gently.

Nicole put down the remains of her roll. "Not remotely," she groaned, rubbing her aching forehead. "I . . . well, I just found out I was completely deluded, all right? In fact, this entire U.S. Girls thing has brought me nothing but misery from start to finish. Do you think it's easy losing this much weight? And then to have Leah win the contest in St. Louis instead of me! I mean, it was *my* contest. Not to mention that Courtney isn't even speaking to me because I got invited and she didn't. She wanted me to stay home with her, and I really wish I had because—"

Nicole stopped herself abruptly, belatedly aware she was talking too much. "Well, let's just say this whole thing has been a disaster. When I started out, I actually thought God was sending me here to make me a model, and now I'm not even sure I want to be one. It's weird, but I think I actually had more fun the day I hung out at the youth rally."

Guy didn't speak right away, but when at last he broke the silence his words astonished her.

"Then maybe God *did* want you to come to L.A.," he said. "Just not for the reason you thought."

Nicole felt her mouth hanging open, but she was too dumbfounded to shut it. Was *that* the sign God was sending? That she *wasn't* supposed to be a model?

Guy stood up and collected his trash. "Well, I'd better get back to my room before my friends start thinking I'm lost. Maybe I'll see you around when we get home."

"Sure," she said dully, knowing a kiss-off when she heard one. She was positive Guy had no intention of looking her up back in Clearwater Crossing, and she'd never run into him otherwise. Even so, he *had* kind of helped her . . . and she didn't want to seem immature.

Again.

"I'll see you later," she agreed, trying to smile. But, watching him walk off across the lobby, she made herself face reality. *I'll never see him again.*

The two of them had come a long way from that first blind date, when she'd thought she was too cool for him. Now she knew better.

Now he was too cool for her.

Melanie walked out of the elevator alone, headed toward her hotel room. Leah and Jenna were still downstairs, talking to the other two members of Guy's band, and Melanie had planned to use the opportunity to beat Jenna into the shower. But when she turned the corner, Brad was leaning against her door, waiting for her.

Contrasting with his black leather jacket, his blond hair framed his face like a halo, and in his hand was a single red rose. He held it out to her as she approached.

"I told you I'd see you again," he said with a happy smile.

"How did you know where my room was?"

"Ah, I know many things," he said with a silly fake accent.

Of course he did, she realized. He worked for the hotel.

She held his flower to her nose, trying all the while to block the memory of the last red rose she'd

185

received—from Jesse. At the time she'd been so angry with him for taping it to her locker, potentially exposing their relationship, that she'd never even thanked him for it. Now, her face hidden in Brad's rose, she wished she had handled that differently.

"Thank you," she said, sorry her words couldn't count for both flowers.

He smiled. "I'm parked outside."

"What? No way! It's too late to go anywhere now."

"Come on," he said. "Just one last drive, for old times' sake."

Part of her wanted to stand her ground, to say she was too tired. But he looked so adorable standing there, grinning.

"Well . . . maybe a short one," she relented.

They drove down Sunset and Hollywood Boulevards, retracing their first night's route. Brad was as handsome as ever, but somehow the appeal of the city had already faded. And by the time Brad's car pulled back into the hotel parking lot, Melanie thought she knew why. She missed home. California had been fun, but she was glad to be leaving for Missouri the next morning.

Brad picked a dark parking place and switched off the engine. "So. I guess this is finally good-bye."

Melanie nodded. "I guess it is."

"Can I call you in Missouri?"

She hadn't expected the question, but she didn't hesitate with her answer. "No."

Brad looked amazed, if not hurt.

"I'm sorry," she added hurriedly. "I didn't mean it like that. But you and I . . . I mean, we're never going to see each other again. What would be the point?"

"Why does there have to be a point? Why can't we just say hello?"

"I'd rather remember this the way it ended—as a perfect weekend."

"Just because the weekend is over doesn't mean we have to be. I know it's pretty long-distance, but . . ." He looked at her hopefully.

"It's just, well, there's kind of someone else," she said, barely able to believe the words tumbling from her mouth.

"What?" Brad exclaimed. "Why didn't you say so before?"

*Good question*, she thought, scrambling for a reason.

"This is going to sound kind of stupid," she said slowly. "But I really didn't know. I mean I didn't until now."

Brad pushed his hair off his face with both hands. "Oh, so being around me convinced you? That makes me feel really good."

"It's not like that. Well, it kind of is—but not because you did anything wrong. It's just, well . . . this guy, Jesse. I thought he drove me crazy, but now that I've broken up with him he's all I think about."

"Sounds crazy, all right," Brad said sulkily.

"It's not that you're not great," she said, desperate to explain. "In fact, it's probably just the opposite. I really like you, Brad. And if a guy like *you* can't get Jesse out of my head, well . . . I guess I'm not as finished with him as I thought."

She hesitated, out of things to say. "I'm sorry," she added lamely.

"So am I."

Reaching across the car, she took his hand. "Does it really matter? I mean, if we lived in the same town, maybe things would be different, but tonight was the end for us anyway. I'm only saying let's end it clean."

"Is that what you told that other guy?"

Melanie drew in her breath, embarrassed. "Now that you mention it . . . yes."

But, to her surprise, Brad grinned. "Good. So then there's still hope for me, too. If I'm ever in Missouri, I'll look you up."

Melanie laughed. "How do you think you'll find me?" she teased.

"Listen, if I can find a speck on the map like Clearwater Crossing, then finding you will be easy. One high school, right?"

Melanie gestured from the top of his head to his knees, a game show hostess with a prize. "All this and brains too!" she said before she turned serious again.

"I will miss you, Brad. And I'll always remember this weekend."

Moving her hands to his broad shoulders, she

leaned forward to kiss him good-bye. Brad's arms closed around her tightly, but even as their lips met, Melanie's thoughts were already on a plane back to Missouri.

"Good-bye, Brad," she whispered, slipping out of his car.

Jesse was far from perfect, but somehow he'd gotten farther under her skin than she'd ever imagined. She walked through the parking lot toward the hotel, wondering what she'd say to him when they met again.

*One thing's pretty clear: I owe him a major apology.* Her heart beat a little faster.

*And I really hope he'll take it.*

# Sixteen

It still seemed absurdly early on Tuesday morning when Jenna heard the hall door of the next room slam. A split second later Leah poked her head through the connecting doorway.

"Did anyone call up here yet?" she asked frantically.

"You mean anyone like the shuttle?" Jenna let go of the backpack she was stuffing to check her watch again. "Relax. We have thirty more minutes."

"Easy for you to say—you're already packed. Where are Melanie and Nicole?"

Jenna nodded toward the bathroom. "Melanie's in the shower, and I think Nicole went down to the gift shop. She said she'd be right back."

"Great," Leah grumbled. "She'd better hurry."

Turning toward her own room, Leah snatched her suitcase off the floor, slammed it open, and began throwing clothes into it from the hotel dresser. Jenna drifted over to watch the frenzied packing from the doorway her friend had just vacated.

"So did you sign whatever it was the judges wanted?" Jenna asked. "Are you done with them now?"

Her question brought a smile to Leah's lips.

"I am *so* done with them! Good-bye, U.S. Girls, and good riddance!" Leah lifted a pile of dirty laundry off the floor and dropped it into her suitcase, stuffing it down to make more room.

"Get this," she said. "I'm down there signing their final releases, right? And that judge Nicole and I talked to at the party tells me that my essay was what killed me. I mean, he practically came right out and said I'd have won with a more 'corporate' essay."

"That's awful!" Jenna exclaimed. "What a horrible thing to say."

Leah shook her head. "Who cares? I couldn't be more out of here."

She seemed sincere, but Jenna knew how much faith Leah put in her own intelligence. Losing because of her essay really had to hurt.

"I guess, in a way, there is a bright side, though," Jenna said slowly. "Most models don't write essays, so if you just wanted to model on your own—I mean, with an agency or something—it sounds like you'd be able to. In fact, who knows? You might even make more money that way than the scholarship was worth."

Leah looked up from her packing, her expression alarmed. "That's *not* going to happen. And if you breathe so much as a syllable of that idea to Nicole, I swear I'll—"

"Never mind," Jenna said quickly, laughing. "I can see where this is going."

The bathroom faucet shut off with a clunk. Melanie had finished her shower.

"I'd better finish my packing," Jenna said. "I still have a couple more things."

"Then go. Pack. I'm not missing that shuttle for anything."

Jenna returned to the backpack on her bed and checked through what she'd put in so far to make sure she hadn't forgotten something. Then, very carefully, she put Kei Kulani's autograph on top, two stiff sheets of taped-together cardboard keeping it flat and safe. When she had finished, there was just enough room for her final item: the Fire & Water T-shirts she'd bought for Caitlin and Peter. Jenna had rolled them into fat little sausages tied with curly ribbons, and she wanted to keep them on top for immediate giving.

*I can't wait to see them!* she thought as she zipped the pack closed over the shirts, trying to ignore her worries about how Caitlin might react to her.

Still . . .

*You never know. Maybe she's forgiven me already.*

If not, Jenna wouldn't rest until she'd re-earned her sister's trust.

Despite the extremely late hour in Missouri, she and Leah had both made calls home the night before—Leah to report on the contest and Jenna on the concert. The whole time Jenna had been talking to her mother, though, she'd really been dying to ask for Caitlin. But everyone had been in bed, and since there was no way of knowing whether Caitlin would even have come to the phone, Jenna had chickened out. Why risk alerting her mom to a problem she seemed to know nothing about? No, it was better to fix things in person—and that was just what she meant to do the second she got home.

*I wonder if Peter's had a chance to find out if David likes Caitlin yet,* Jenna mused as she carried her backpack to the door. The thought froze her in place partway across the room.

*Oops. None of your business,* she reminded herself sternly. *Don't even go there.*

"Yes, yes. I'm coming," Melanie replied, feeling blindly around in her fully packed suitcase. "Just give me two more seconds."

The way Leah was riding herd on them all, anyone would think she was the only person in a hurry to get back to Clearwater Crossing.

"I'm going to go down and make sure the shuttle doesn't leave without us," Leah said.

"Good idea." Melanie thought Leah was being paranoid about getting left behind, but if paranoia bought her a minute of peace she was all in favor of it.

Leah withdrew her head from the connecting door and shut it.

"I'll go with her," Jenna said, picking up her own luggage and the extra bag she'd been assigned by Nicole. "See you downstairs?"

"I'll be right there."

But the moment Jenna was gone, Melanie opened her suitcase wide to get a better look at its contents.

"Okay. That looks all right," she muttered under her breath.

The print she had bought for Jesse was still right in the center where she'd put it. She rolled up a couple of shirts anyway and double-padded the corners.

*I hope he likes it*, she thought nervously, trying to imagine how she'd give it to him.

But instead of helping her with that problem, her brain took her straight to the part where Jesse thanked her for the gift. Eyes half closed, she imagined him taking her into his arms the romantic way he'd done on New Year's Eve. A moment later, her heart was pounding as hard as if he were really in the room.

"Okay!" she said, opening her eyes and snapping her suitcase shut. "That's enough of that."

But the slickness of her hand on the doorknob as she left the room betrayed how nervous she really was.

She rode down in the elevator, the butterflies in her stomach defying gravity all the way. Taking a deep breath, she braced herself as the elevator lurched to a stop in the lobby.

*Twenty-four hours from now, my life could be com-*

*pletely different*, she thought as the doors parted. She crossed her fingers.

*Make it so*.


"Is that the shuttle to the airport?" Leah shouted, leaving Jenna and Melanie behind as she bolted over to the doorman. A van had just appeared outside the main entrance.

"Yep, that's it," the doorman said. "Do you need some help with your luggage?"

"*I* don't," Leah said, looking anxiously back toward the elevators.

Sunlight was streaming into the lobby now, hot through the plate glass windows. *Where the heck is Nicole?* When Leah had left their room, Nicole had promised to be down within five minutes.

"One of my friends is upstairs, and I don't know what's keeping her," Leah told the doorman. "I thought we'd brought down enough of her junk, but maybe she still can't carry what's left."

"Don't worry. We won't leave anyone behind. Do you want to call her on the courtesy phone?"

"Yes. All right."

Leah stopped to take a deep breath, determined to pace herself for the long morning still ahead. "You're *sure* that shuttle won't leave?"

"Not a chance," the doorman promised. "I won't let it."

Jenna and Melanie had caught up by then and stood listening to the conversation.

"Go ahead," Jenna urged. "We'll get this stuff loaded."

Leah crossed the polished floor toward the nearest courtesy phone, reassured. They were as good as on their way.

Reaching for the ring around her neck, she twisted it through her shirt as she walked.

*I wonder if Miguel will be at the airport,* she thought.

It didn't seem likely, considering that that Tuesday was a school day. But *she* was missing school. It could definitely be done.

She imagined him meeting her at the gate, folding her into his arms. . . .

And if he did, she knew what her answer would be.

"One more minute," Nicole promised, hanging up the phone.

Everyone else was down in the lobby. The shuttle was waiting. Leah was coming unglued.

But Nicole wasn't ready to go yet. After everything that had happened over the past three days, it seemed there had to be something more. Some last-minute revelation, some newfound resolution . . .

She had purposely lagged behind the others, wanting to be the last one left in the room.

*Sort of to bid the dream good-bye, I guess.*

Tears rose again at the thought, but somehow she managed to blink them back. *If what I've seen this*

196

*weekend is what modeling's all about, then maybe it's just as well.*

Still, it was hard.

Nicole carried her last bag to the door and put it out in the hall with the others before stepping back inside for one final look at the room. So much luxury . . .

*I guess it was fun while it lasted.*

She had no idea what she'd do with her life if she wasn't going to be a model. She felt lost at the mere prospect. Even so, it seemed like time to move on.

With a long, deep breath and a toss of her head, Nicole stalked out of the hotel room, letting the door bang shut behind her.

**Find out what happens next in Clearwater Crossing #10, *No Doubt*.**

## About the Author

Laura Peyton Roberts holds an M.A. in English from San Diego State University. A native Californian, she lives with her husband in San Diego.

# Real life. Real friends. Real faith.

Clearwater Crossing—where
friendships are formed, hearts
come together, choices have
consequences, and lives
are changed
forever . . .